IN BED
with the
COMPETITION

OTHER BOOKS BY J.K. COI
WRITING AS CHLOE JACOBS

THE MYCLENA CHRONICLES SERIES

Greta and the Goblin King

Greta and the Glass Kingdom

Debbie!

IN BED
with the
COMPETITION

Enjoy!

J.K. Coi

This book is a work of fiction. Names, characters, places, and incidents are the product of the author's imagination or are used fictitiously. Any resemblance to actual events, locales, or persons, living or dead, is coincidental.

Copyright © 2014 by Kristina Coi. All rights reserved, including the right to reproduce, distribute, or transmit in any form or by any means. For information regarding subsidiary rights, please contact the Publisher.

Entangled Publishing, LLC
2614 South Timberline Road
Suite 109
Fort Collins, CO 80525
Visit our website at www.entangledpublishing.com.

Edited by Tracy Montoya and Kate Fall
Cover design by Heather Howland

Manufactured in the United States of America

First Edition June 2014

For Carlo, always.

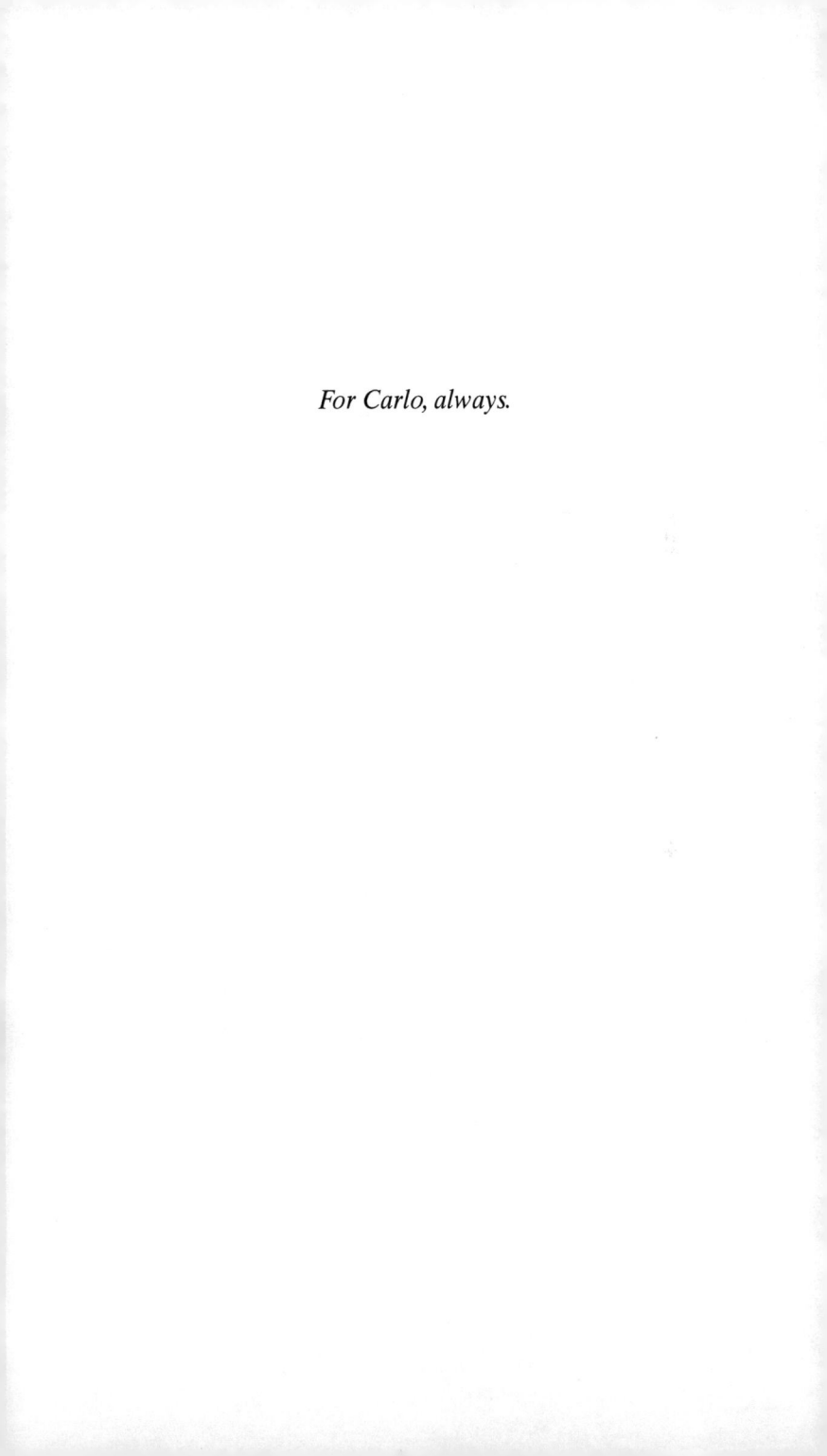

Chapter One

Ben Harrison had seen his fair share of women in bikinis, but this one seemed different. For one, she wasn't model thin with toothpicks for limbs, but had killer curves and legs that went for miles. His mouth went dry as he took it all in. A wide straw hat. The thin ribbon ties of her top coming together in the middle of her back. The ends trailing down a few inches, drawing the eye to the curve of her waist and then lower, to bright red bottoms.

He felt guilty for staring and averted his gaze, but Nolan's low whistle of appreciation reflected Ben's sentiments exactly.

He turned to his friend with a raised brow. "What are *you* looking at?"

Nolan leaned up on one elbow and tilted his sunglasses down the bridge of his nose. "The same thing as you, I'm thinking."

"Well, you can just lie back down and forget about it. We might be here a couple of days early, but there's still a lot to do to get ready for the convention." Ben enjoyed the occasional break, which is why he and his business partner Steve Nolan had come to Antigua two days before this convention was scheduled to begin. But no matter where he went, he never left the work entirely behind, because he still hadn't achieved his goals.

"Not for me," Nolan protested with a grin. "And not for you, either. We got this nailed, Harrison. Everyone will be lining up to hand over their money. And you have to admit, if you look at any more reports, you're going to go blind. Trust me, nobody likes a squinting playboy without a tan, no matter how innovative he is."

Ben frowned. A year ago he'd been a nobody, fighting tooth and nail to make his mark along with all the rest, but after appearing at a few gala events with heiress and model-turned-CEO Meredith Stone, someone had decided to run a story on him, and suddenly he was considered a playboy. "It's bad enough I get that shit from the media. I don't need to hear it from you, too."

"What? You don't appreciate the attention?" Nolan smirked.

It was disconcerting and inconvenient, but Nolan was of the opinion that a little media attention of any kind was a good thing. It had the potential to translate into the kind of corporate interest they desperately needed, and that made it worth putting up with for a while. Both of them had sunk everything they had into their cutting-edge software development company, but it just wasn't enough. They needed more capital, and they needed it *now*.

That's what had brought them to Antigua. The Artificial Intelligence world was a small one, all the industry players would be at this convention, and they would all be looking for the next big Internet money-maker—that's where Optimus Inc. came in.

Nolan grinned. "If you ask me, the fact that the media hounds have locked onto someone else's scent for a while is fucking fantastic."

"Yeah, I'm sure you're ecstatic," Ben answered with a shake of his head.

The reporters might suddenly consider Ben Harrison's life fodder for their pages, but they practically wet themselves over any chance to photograph brilliant mathematician and bad boy Steve Nolan, whose family had been the stuff of society legend until it all fell apart in a public scandal a few years ago…and who was now having too damn much fun at Ben's expense.

Ben's attention shifted back to the woman on the pool deck. She faced away from them, having arranged herself on an available deck chair in front of the sparkling pool. She was applying lotion to her legs and thighs. Her motions were slow and smooth, the sun bouncing off her perfect, slick skin. It didn't take much for him to start imagining those legs wrapped around him…

Maybe he *had* been staring at reports too long. After all, he'd left New York early to scratch his itch for adventure…and a reckless island fling could be exactly the thing he needed.

Nolan moved to get out of his chair. "Well, since you're not going over there, I think I'll introduce myself—"

"No way." Ben shoved him back. He stood and grabbed his shirt, flinging it over his shoulder. "You've got your wish.

I'll clock out for the rest of the day, but that means you have to check in with Clarissa in New York."

Nolan groaned good-naturedly. "Where are you going?"

"Don't worry about me." He glanced over his shoulder. "With any luck, I'll soon be sufficiently distracted for the rest of the night."

Ben walked away, but having escaped Nolan, he quickly changed his mind, deciding he was going back to his room after all. He didn't want to intrude on the woman's privacy. There was going to be a preponderance of a certain type of person at the resort this week: execs and programmers specializing in programming initiatives, and the marketing bottom feeders who were just looking to capitalize on someone else's innovation. The facilities had been completely booked by the convention, so while he couldn't picture many software engineers who looked like her, it stood to reason she was another early arrival taking advantage of an opportunity for some time to relax before the hordes descended, and he didn't want to encroach on that.

As he passed her chair, though, he couldn't help but slow. A large beach bag rested on the ground beside her, a colorful towel spilling out of it. He wondered if she planned to take a dip in the pool later. That was something he didn't think he'd want to miss out on.

Right now, she lounged back in the reclined deck chair. Her drop dead gorgeous body was presented to the sun like an offering, and the front of her was equally as stunning as the rest. The round globes of her breasts teased him from behind smallish triangles of bright red Lycra. Her skin was smooth and creamy, gleaming with the layer of sunscreen she'd just applied, but pale, as if she took vacation about as often as he did. Then again, after a few days in that tiny bikini, she'd be golden in no time.

She'd taken out a book, presumably from the depths of the large bag, but it lay closed in her lap. He raised his brows. That was some dense, technical subject matter. His first instinct had been correct; she was obviously here for the convention. That put a different spin on his interest, and he stopped walking altogether, trying to decide if he recognized her. He thought he might, but oversize dark glasses covered her eyes.

She wore a thick gold band on her thumb that looked better suited to a man, but no rings on any of her other fingers, including the third finger of her left hand. Not that such an absence meant as much these days as it used to. The band gave him pause, though. He used to know someone who wore a thumb ring like that.

Looking closer, he tried to see past the floppy straw hat. It covered her face and hair, with a red ribbon that matched her bikini. Thick curls escaped from beneath it and fell to her shoulders. He used to know someone with tight curls like that, too.

"Um, excuse me. You're in my sun."

He was startled by her relaxed, husky voice, as if she'd just been through a long night of steamy sex, and he was the man who'd awakened her with kisses to do it all over again. That voice was familiar, too.

Very familiar.

He cleared his throat and inclined his head with his most approachable smile. "My apologies. You caught me daydreaming."

"Oh, is that what you were doing? Not staring at my… uh…hat?" Her lips were coated with some kind of clear gloss that made them look wet and full. A cocked eyebrow rose above the rim of her sunglasses. The way she did that, the tilt of her head as she looked up at him…

He laughed, but his gut tightened. "Ah, maybe you're right, and that's what got me daydreaming. You have a very lovely…*hat* after all."

The hair was different. Her body was different…or maybe he'd just never seen so much of it before. If only he could look into her eyes to know for sure.

He readjusted the shirt he'd thrown over his shoulder and stepped closer. "Would you and your hat care to meet me in the bar tonight for a drink?"

That eyebrow went up again at his boldness, and her hand clenched on the book in her lap like a shield.

"I don't mean to intrude on your holiday," he added quickly. "But if you're here alone and you'd like some company…"

She pressed her lips together, and he felt the weight of her assessing gaze travelling down the length of him, even though he couldn't see past the barrier of her dark sunglasses.

After a long moment, she reached up and slid the glasses down the bridge of her nose, revealing deep green eyes. Green like the tropical water surrounding the island.

Her gaze was the same as a physical touch to his skin. Hot and unexpectedly jarring. Those eyes.

Yes. He *knew* those eyes.

He knew *her*.

In the time it took for him to verify his suspicion about her identity, her smile turned brittle, and her expression hardened. "It's only been a little over a year, Harrison. Don't tell me I was *that* forgettable."

Chapter Two

"*Beth.*"

She winced. He was the only person who'd ever gotten away with calling her that. Her brother had tried once, and she'd nearly decked him, but for some reason she'd never objected when Ben had done it.

He sounded so surprised. Yes, she'd changed in the year since seeing him last. She'd let her hair grow out and lost some weight—okay, a lot of weight—but it wasn't like she was a different person.

Anger flared…or was the heat building inside her something else entirely? She couldn't take her eyes of those pecs, unless it was to stare at his abs.

Put your damn shirt on, she wanted to scream. That was the only way she'd be able to concentrate. Of course, *he* hadn't changed at all. He was still too distracting for his own good.

You're concentrating just fine, Liz. Yeah, but she didn't

want to concentrate on *him*. She didn't want to concentrate on the wide expanse of his shoulders, the bulk of his chest, and the grin still curling his damned lips. Or the way his blue eyes glimmered like sunshine bouncing off the water in the pool. She hated that his voice started a fluttery thing way down in the pit of her stomach, and that she couldn't help but notice how his black and red swimming trunks hung low on his waist, showing off more muscle than a man had a right to have.

She definitely did *not* want to admit that her heart had leapt into her throat when he'd stopped in front of her.

"What are you doing here, Harrison? Aren't you much too busy going to dinner parties with society heiresses for a boring industry convention these days?"

He only crossed his arms over that massive chest—which did unexpectedly exciting and traitorous things to her insides.

She had the sudden urge to stand up from the deck chair to give herself some height, but since she was only five-foot-five in her short-heeled beach sandals, he would still be looking way down at her.

"I didn't recognize you for a minute there," he said, gaze dipping down again. "It's nice to see you." His voice lowered.

Go figure, he actually sounded sincere.

If he took off his sunglasses, what would she see? Welcome or nuisance? Indifference or regret? Had he thought about her at all? Did he think about what had happened between them, or was it all a wash? Forgotten in the excitement of his new venture…and dates with famous women?

"I wish I could say the same." She readjusted her sunglasses so he couldn't read anything from her eyes. He'd always said that all he had to do was look into her eyes to know what she was thinking.

Well, he could try to figure her out all he wanted, but the last year had been filled with changes, and she'd learned a lot, including how to perfect her poker face.

She purposely picked up her book, thinking he'd take the hint and go away.

Just as she realized the book was upside down and hastened to flip it over, he came closer, blocking out the sun with his to-die-for physique.

The sudden shade didn't cool her body down. As he closed the distance between them, she only got hotter.

She held her breath as he dragged another lounger across the pool deck until it was right beside hers.

He repeated his invitation. "Have a drink with me."

Her mouth dropped open. "Why the hell would I do that?"

"Because we should talk."

"I've been in the same place with the same phone number. If you wanted to *talk*, you knew very well how to reach me every day of the last fourteen months." She winced at the hint of bitterness in her voice. She couldn't really blame him for not keeping in touch. He'd moved across the country and started his own company, and since she'd gone into business for herself as well, she knew what a huge, time-consuming undertaking it must have been. Not to mention that they hadn't exactly gone their separate ways on the best of terms.

"Are you saying you're busy then? What else do you have to do tonight?"

As if she couldn't possibly have anything better to do on

an island paradise than spend the evening with him?

Dropping the book to her lap, she crossed her arms in front of her, but wasn't deluded that she was any better protected from his piercing looks and disarmingly familiar smile.

"Not that it's any of your business, but I came here for work, not to waste my time tramping down memory lane with the likes of you."

"Are you pitching something?" His expression narrowed. With competitive calculation or simply interest?

Wouldn't you like to know? In college he'd been the only person to get better grades than her. The only person to get more attention from their professors. He'd gotten a scholarship she had applied for. A job she'd wanted. When he left for New York, she'd thought she was done competing with him, but she'd done her research and had no delusions. Their two companies were producing a very similar product, and being forced to compete with Ben again had been bound to happen sooner or later, despite the geographic distance that was now between them.

Yes, Liz knew exactly the kind of competition she was up against at this convention and in this industry on the whole. The same competition she'd always been up against.

Ben Harrison.

I'm not discussing my business with you," she said stubbornly.

"That's fine," he said too easily. "We don't have to talk business."

"There's nothing else we could possibly discuss with each other."

"Beth, we were friends for three years, and it's been

over a year since I saw you. Is it so difficult to believe that I just want to know how you've been?"

She looked away and pretended to be captivated by the beauty of the pristine pool.

Yes, they'd been friends, and the good-natured competitiveness between them had always been grounded in respect and an admiration for one another's intelligence and abilities.

Ben had been a good friend...a great friend...her *best* friend...right up until the moment he'd suggested they go into business together, and then, just to make matters even worse...he'd kissed her.

No matter how hard she'd tried to get them back to their friendship place, it hadn't been the same after that. And when he left for New York a month later—alone—it had almost been a relief, because she knew she'd never be able to banish the other feelings he'd forced her to acknowledge, the ones that stripped her raw and left her vulnerable.

How could he do that? How could he just ruin everything? Shock and denial had left her shaken, angry, and scared for a long time, but she'd refused to admit she might be angry with herself, too. Because part of her had seen it coming, part of her had wanted it so badly...but she *never* would have risked it.

She dared a glance back at him. The sight of all that sculpted male flesh and those strong, capable hands sent shivers racing through her even now. Her mouth went dry, and her nipples tightened.

"Eight o'clock in the bar?" he said expectantly. He appeared calm, relaxed, and *criminally* good looking.

She shouldn't. Corporate secrets were stolen every day

in her industry. She needed to protect herself, especially from him. She remembered well how competitive Ben could be, and they no longer had friendship between them to protect her from his ruthless business practices.

"All right. I'll have a drink with you."

His smile was radiant as he stood, his big body casting a shadow again. "Good. I'll see you tonight at the bar then?"

She nodded slowly, transfixed by the sight of those flexing arms and rippling abs as he pulled his T-shirt over his head and tugged it down, covering everything—and yet not covering enough, because the shirt molded to him like a second skin.

Good God. Are you seriously thinking what I think you're thinking? He's going to eat you up and spit you out.

Watching him walk away, she clenched her jaw and imagined exactly how the "eating up" part might play out.

Chapter Three

What happens in Antigua…

Liz shook her head at the reckless thought. Back in her room out of the hot sun, her common sense had started to return in a rush.

She might be here on business, but the temptation to use her trip to the beautiful tropical island to indulge in a rare opportunity for some hot and sexy fun in the sun had occurred to her even before running into Harrison at the pool. It was why she'd arrived a couple of days before the convention was scheduled to start.

Not that she would really do anything with a stranger. That would be rash and reckless, and Liz was anything but. She was always the responsible one, the one who made plans, who avoided confrontation. In fact, starting her own business was the most reckless thing she'd ever done, and making that decision had given her ulcers.

No, she'd never have a fling with a stranger.

But Ben Harrison wasn't exactly a stranger, now was he? *With him? That's just asking for trouble.*

She took a deep breath and gave herself a disapproving look in the bathroom mirror. "That's why it's just a drink, nothing else."

Her brain was telling her not to be such an idiot as she worried her bottom lip with her teeth. Then again, lower, where it counted, she felt a rush of warmth, and anticipation surged through her bloodstream.

"Just one drink," she reminded herself again sternly.

She peeled the towel from her wet hair and gently rubbed the ends. The terrycloth felt stiff and a bit scratchy, like it had been washed in too much bleach. "One drink because we used to be friends. One drink to prove I'm a professional, and that he can't intimidate me."

She nodded firmly.

Her cell phone rang, buzzing along across the countertop beside her makeup case. She dropped the towel and checked the number, then cradled the phone to her ear. "Hi, Daniel. Are you feeling better?" Her brother didn't travel well, and there'd been turbulence on the flight. After settling into their rooms, Daniel had wanted to rest.

"Liz, I just heard Benjamin Harrison is going to be here."

"Yes, I know. I saw him a little while ago."

"You talked to him?"

"Yes, listen. This is a big industry event. It was always within the realm of possibility that he would want to make an appearance," she said. "But it'll be fine."

"How can it be fine? In business for only a year and he's already left a trail of broken and bleeding start-ups lying in his wake. The man has a knack for partnering up with specialists who have intellectual property or a skill set that he wants, sucking them dry, and then leaving them in the dust without a second thought." Her brother's voice was getting higher and more agitated by the moment. "I heard that he and his partner are trolling for investors now. And you know they'll be hitting up Diego Vargas." Diego Vargas was known to be a down-to-earth professional who ran his company with integrity and intelligence.

"That doesn't automatically mean that they're going to win and we're going to lose."

"Have you *met* the guy Harrison is working with? We're so screwed. Apparently, Steve Nolan has got connections with everyone."

"That's no guarantee of anything." Her head ached. She'd spent years trying to help her brother overcome the damage done to his self-esteem by their childhood, but it remained an ongoing battle, and sometimes she got so tired of always being the strong, steady one in the family.

"But—"

"We've worked hard, and our program is flawless," she reminded him sternly. "This is our chance to show people what we have to offer. Once they see it, we won't have any trouble getting Vargas interested, and it won't matter what Ben Harrison and his partner have up their sleeves."

Daniel seemed overly concerned about this development, but the truth was he might be right to worry. Diego Vargas was the president of Jemarcho Inc., a company with deep pockets and huge marketing needs. Her company's AI software, which she'd designed to strategically analyze online search results and other criteria in order to independently adapt specific marketing tools and initiate more effective campaigns, would be perfect for Jemarcho. But since Sharkston Co. was still getting its feet wet, it would take a lot to wow him. If Harrison got there first…

"So, what did he say to you?"

"He didn't say anything. He barely even recognized me." That was mostly true. Granted, on top of her weight loss and new hair, she'd also been wearing dark glasses at the time, and the ghostlike quality of her near nakedness had probably blinded him for a minute. Now she wished she'd gone to that tanning salon to get a "base coat" like Sarah had suggested.

Liz wondered what her friend and office manager would have said about Ben inviting her to have drinks tonight. That was a no-brainer. Sarah was ten times bolder than Liz. She would have said, *Go for it*.

Liz looked in the bathroom mirror as heat flooded her cheeks.

"So what are we going to do?" Daniel asked. He obviously wasn't going to calm down easily.

"We're not doing anything."

"Are you serious? Liz, we have to—"

"No, listen to me. I agree he would probably love it if just his presence distracted us, but we can't let him get under our skin. We have a plan, and we're going to stick to it. Let's not do anything reckless. Let's not make things easier for him by being off our game. All right?"

"I'm sorry. I guess you're right. I just don't want anything to jeopardize our chances with Vargas."

"Jemarcho Inc. isn't our only option," she reminded him. He'd been so focused on making this deal lately, he reminded her of their father. No wonder she had ulcers.

"But it's the best. You said it yourself."

True, but they couldn't put all their eggs in one basket. Trying to explain that to Daniel, though, was like trying to teach logic to an inch worm. He was so focused on the money they needed, she sometimes felt that was all he cared about, that the company itself was just another poker table for him to play at.

He grew quiet on the other end of the line. Her frustration with him turned to guilt. He had a gift for sending her on an emotional rollercoaster, but she knew he didn't do it on purpose. He'd been in a constant struggle with a gambling addiction since his late teens, and it had been an uphill battle to keep it under control. More than once she'd had to bail him out of trouble, and he'd fallen off the wagon again about fourteen months ago. It had ruined his relationship with his last girlfriend when she found out that all the money they'd been saving to buy a house was gone, sending him into an emotional tailspin darker than anything she'd seen from him before.

Liz had been forced to cash in every cent she'd been saving up for Sharkston Co. to cover his debt and help him get into another recovery program, but this time it had been different. Since the program, he'd been withdrawn, defensive, and he refused to talk to her about anything besides work—and even when it came to that, she'd been hard-pressed to get his input.

"Hey," she said. "Everything's going to be fine. *We're* going to be fine."

"Yeah, you're right. I know." He sighed.

She rubbed her temple. She always got a headache dealing with her baby brother. It was amazing how trouble zeroed in on him like a heat-seeking missile...and that the fallout of the resulting explosion always ended up in her lap. That was no doubt a product of having two parents so focused on their careers that their children had always come a close second—sometimes third or fourth—in priority. Even when her parents had been alive, Liz was the one who ended up taking care of herself and her brother, because their parents were always working, or arguing about who was going to have to waste their valuable time doing things like feeding the children or taking them to the doctor.

Frowning into the mirror at the sight of her rapidly drying hair starting to frizz up into a halo around her head, she shook off the bitterness of the past and focused on the future. The somewhat pressing, immediate future.

"Listen, I—I have some plans tonight, so why don't I call you in the morning after breakfast? I'm going to see if they plan to set up an early registration table for the convention."

"You're going out?" He sounded surprised and a little wounded, making Liz wince. Usually she was the one waiting at home with a light on while her brother went out on the town. But surprisingly, she hadn't changed her mind about going out to meet Ben. "I thought we could read over those portfolios once more," he said. "Order in room service and—"

"It's a good idea, but there's nothing there we haven't already gone over a hundred times. We're ready, Daniel. Everything is in order."

"Are you sure you're okay? You never think we're ready. You always want to triple check everything right up to the last second." He paused. "Are you meeting someone?"

She cleared her throat. "Ah...I'm having a drink with Ben."

"*What*? You're not serious?" His incredulity came right through her cell phone. "After everything we just talked about?"

"We might be business rivals, but that doesn't mean we can't be civil." Was she trying to convince Daniel...or herself? "Don't worry, I can handle this. I can handle Ben Harrison."

Glancing back up into the mirror, she tried not to see the lie in her own eyes.

Chapter Four

Ben stopped in the entrance of the busy, darkened bar. It was already eight fifteen. A last-minute call had him running late for his date with Beth. As a result, his hair was still damp from the shower, making the collar of his shirt wet too, so that it clung to his neck.

What if she took his lateness as an insult and had already left? Worse yet, what if she didn't show up at all?

Does it really matter that much?

Yes. Not that he was willing to examine the reasons why.

He'd very consciously decided *not* to think about Elizabeth Carlson often during the last year, but now that he'd seen her again, he hadn't been able to stop. The memories were too close, too sharp. Her image wouldn't leave him. It was burned into his brain.

After years of friendship, things between them had fallen apart when he left Seattle, and he'd wondered what he would feel if he ever saw her again.

His gaze locked on the beauty by the bar. Now he knew.

She was all the way on the opposite side of the room, but he would have picked her out at three times the distance. In fact, he wasn't likely to mistake that figure of hers ever again and couldn't believe it had actually taken him a minute to recognize her earlier.

Out on the pool deck, his body had responded just like any guy's would when confronted with a hot chick in a bikini. But that was nothing compared to the moment he'd recognized those sea green eyes and her name had popped out of his mouth. The physical response had become a hundred times more powerful. It had taken all of his control to sound calm and cool in the face of her radiant beauty.

She'd always been gorgeous and brilliant, but there had been a definite off-limits vibe coming from her while they'd been friends. He'd crossed the boundary once in desperation and it had changed everything between them.

Trying it again had a good chance of having the same effect—or worse—but he wasn't sure that was going to stop him. He'd always had a pathological unwillingness to accept failure—not that he wanted to explore the roots of that—and he also liked the adrenaline rush he got from taking risks. He had no doubt that they'd be amazing in bed together, and if he could convince her of as much, maybe he'd finally get her out of his system.

A gentle spotlight glowed down on her. She looked absolutely stunning in a clingy, turquoise wrap thing that cascaded all the way to her ankles. It didn't have any straps to go over her shoulders. Either there was some secret to the design, or she was relying on nothing but her own natural curves to hold it up. Curves shown to perfection by the contrast of her creamy skin against the bold color of her dress.

She'd pulled those thick, shiny red curls up into some kind of arty twist at the top of her head, leaving the nape of her neck bare. Long dangly jewelry hung from her ears and brushed her shoulders, sparkling silver under the lights.

Men flanked her, but she didn't pay them any attention. She leaned over the bar and said something to the bartender, who smiled and dropped an elbow on the counter, leaning over it to respond.

Seeing her answering smile to whatever smooth line the bartender was giving her, Ben started making his way toward her.

The smile on her face froze when she looked up and saw him. She pulled her little purse tight to her belly, making him feel like a predator, with her as the sweet little thing he'd sink his teeth into. He didn't know how he felt about that, but the smile stretching his lips definitely felt wolfish. He poured every ounce of charm he had into it. If he were smart, he would do his best to turn that anxiousness of hers into soft, biddable need, melt her defences, and sweetly pry all her corporate secrets from her.

He bit back the bitter taste of disgust. He wasn't that guy anymore. As much as he would have stopped at nothing to break down a competitor not too long ago, that had changed. *He* had changed.

He re-pasted the smile on his face. He didn't want to take Beth off guard or hammer away her defenses. He didn't want to sucker her.

He knew exactly what he *did* want from her, though, and he was going to prove that she wanted it too.

...

She'd felt a sizzle in the air, glanced up, and had somehow known she would find him watching her.

He crossed the room, walking through the crowd as if no one stood between them. She was being pursued, hunted. And all the arguing she'd done with herself earlier started up again in her head.

"Sorry I'm late, but I'm glad you waited for me." He stopped in front of her and leaned in close, making her heart race.

His lips ghosted against the sensitive spot just beneath her jaw, and a shiver went down her spine. She had to press her lips together to keep from betraying herself with a gasp. When he straightened and took her hand, her breath hitched as he brought it to his mouth, even though he barely touched her.

"You were only a few minutes late." She gently pulled her fingers back with a quiver of excitement.

The smile he bestowed on her would have stopped traffic. She didn't think she could take too many of those without her defenses crumbling completely. Already, she felt shaky. In the face of this man's steady confidence and daring demeanor, she was a mouse.

"Well, even so, thank you for waiting," he said gently. "I would have felt horrible if you'd left, thinking I'd forgotten our date."

Renewing her determination to prove he had no effect on her, she thrust her shoulders back and shrugged. "It's not really a date." She gave him her brightest smile. "And there were enough gentlemen offering to keep me company if you decided not to show. I don't think I would have been alone for longer than…oh…a minute or so."

"I have no doubt about that." His gaze turned smoky and penetrating, like he saw all the way through her. This wasn't the Ben Harrison she remembered.

The man she remembered was reckless and daring, overwhelmingly driven and confident—and she had no doubt he'd only compounded on those qualities since moving to New York—but there was a different side to him now too, one she'd only caught brief glimpses of when they'd been friends.

He radiated so much sex appeal and wicked promise tonight that Liz's breathing thinned. She wondered for the hundredth time why she'd agreed to this. It was so unlike her to act against her instincts…and then she glanced at him as he turned away to order a drink, and the answer was obvious.

His dark hair was still damp from a shower, pushed back from his forehead. It was longer than she remembered, carrying a bit of a wave that made him look like a playboy.

Most of the other men in the bar looked stiff and stuffy in their suits and ties as if it was cocktail hour in the city on a Friday night. Ben seemed relaxed and comfortable. He'd adopted the less formal dress code of the islands, pairing tan pants with a fitted black shirt that he'd left open at the collar.

The casual look should have made him appear average, like a normal guy on holiday. But whether Ben was in nothing but swimming trunks, or covered up from head to toe, his presence outshone everyone else. No doubt he could wear denim, walk into a boardroom filled to the rafters with expensive suits, and still make everyone jump to attention.

When he reached across the bar to grab his Heineken from the server, his shirt sleeve rode up to flash a watch that looked more expensive than her car.

"So, it looks like you're doing well. Your new company must be a success?" she blurted, then blushed.

Liz felt the full impact of his piercing, assessing gaze as he turned back to her. "I thought we weren't going to talk business tonight?"

She nodded. "You're right. I just meant…you look good." Having raised her voice to be heard above the background noise, that last part coincided with an unexpected lull in the overall din and came out sounding extra loud, practically echoing between them.

She snorted and smacked a hand over her mouth while Ben chuckled.

She was still smiling as he leaned into her again, probably so he wouldn't have to speak over the crowd that had quickly escalated to its previous, deafening level of noise.

Her heart pounded as she faced him, drowning out everything but the rumble of his voice, a physical thing against her skin. "You look fantastic," he said.

His hand came to rest on the small of her back. The touch was electric.

She froze. Ben froze. His gaze seemed to have locked onto her mouth, making her want to pull her lip between her teeth, making her head spin. Their nearness suddenly seemed too intimate, too close, taking her off guard. The solid weight of his arm was warm against hers, but neither of them moved.

She forced herself to look away and cleared her throat. "How is your mother?" she asked, cowardly retreating to safer ground.

"You mean, you haven't talked to her this week?" He lifted an eyebrow, but the way he looked at her hadn't changed, sending tingles racing up and down her spine. "She told me that you came to see her after I left for New York."

She blushed and focused on a water ring staining the wood grain of the bar in front of her. "Just once or twice, to make sure she wasn't going all empty nest syndrome or anything."

When Liz's father died, she was just starting her first year of college. Daniel stayed with their aunt's family for two years until he finished high school and they didn't have a lot of extra room in their house, so she rarely went "home for the holidays." After she met Ben, he invited her to his mother's place for dinner every once in a while. Even though her and Ben's friendship hadn't been able to survive his move to New York, Liz had given in to the impulse to go see his mother a few times since then, and she could even admit—to herself—that part of the reason she went over there was to hear the news about Ben's successes.

"Well, I appreciate it," he said in a low voice. "And she's doing great. I only wish you had decided to come over during the times I was back home to visit."

She shook her head. "That wouldn't have been a good idea."

"Because you didn't want to see me."

She pressed her lips together, refusing to look up at him. "Because we didn't have anything to say to each other."

A bright and cheerful voice on the other side of her startled both of them, and they jerked from each other like teenagers who'd been caught making out.

If only.

"Hello there! I'm Laura Dunham."

The woman stepped up to the bar between her and Ben with a bright smile. She wore a loosely flowing, floral-print dress with a delicate lace shawl over her shoulders. She would have looked like she belonged in the laid-back heat of Antigua if not for the super smooth, blunt hair style, cut diagonal to her chin, that was more corporate vogue than relaxed island style.

Liz was certain she'd never met Laura Denham, so she was confused as to why the woman had interrupted them. Maybe it was a Caribbean thing. People were friendlier when they were on vacation, right?

With a quick glance at a bemused-looking Ben, she held out her hand with an answering smile. "Hi. It's nice to meet you. I'm Elizabeth."

"Yes, it's nice to meet you too, Ms. Carlson." She turned to Ben with a nod. "And Mr. Harrison."

Ben smiled and shook Laura's hand as well. "I'm sorry, but I don't remember where we've met."

"No, we don't know each other, although I've seen your pictures. Especially yours, Mr. Harrison." The woman chuckled, obviously referring to the recent write-up that had been in *Prestige Magazine*.

Liz was surprised to see an actual blush in Ben's cheeks as he grimaced and said, "I hope you didn't actually read that horrible interview."

"You mean the one that called you the new Playboy CEO of the industry?" Liz said with a teasing laugh.

His lips twisted in a light-hearted grin. "You've been reading about me?"

"I might have skimmed it," she admitted with a delicate cough. "You know…for the *other* articles."

It was a strange moment. The sexual tension between them was still high even with the other woman's presence, but their easy back-and-forth ribbing was just like old times.

Finally, Ben dropped his gaze and turned back to Ms. Denham. "So are you here for the convention, Ms. Denham?"

"Oh, please just call me Laura." She waved off the formality like they were already all close friends. "In fact, I'm this year's convention chair. I was going to speak to each of you tomorrow before registration, but since I noticed you both here tonight, this works just as well. I hope you don't mind the interruption."

"Of course not. What can we do for you?" said Liz.

"Well, I have a bit of a favor to ask."

"Of course, anything you need." She was a little relieved to have a distraction. It gave her a moment to take a step back and breathe. She might have been thinking about Ben constantly since seeing him that afternoon, but it still hadn't prepared her for the way she would feel to spend the evening with him.

"You don't know how happy I am to hear that." Laura clapped her hands together. "Unfortunately, one of our speakers has pulled out of the event. Tyson Wallace of SynServ Technologies has had a scheduling conflict and won't be able to attend."

"That's such a shame," Liz said. "I was especially looking forward to sitting in on his seminar about large-scale distributed deep networks."

Laura nodded. "Yes, he's such a knowledgeable man. His absence will certainly be noted by the attendees. He was supposed to present for us, as well as give the closing luncheon speech." She looked back and forth between Ben and Liz. "But we've come up with a solution, and I hope you'll both be up for it."

"Do you want us to take on the holes this leaves in your seminar schedule?" Ben asked, a gleam in his eyes.

"Oh yes, that would be wonderful." Laura beamed at them both.

Liz would have liked more notice for something like this, to make sure she could prepare properly. But there was no way she could turn it down, because Ben certainly wouldn't.

A little thrill shot through her as it occurred to her that this could be a massive opportunity. Presenting a seminar at this convention was a really big deal, usually reserved for the industry leaders. Mentally, she started flipping through program ideas.

"We also had something else in mind," said Laura. "Something bold and different."

"Oh, what would that be?" Liz asked, curious and excited.

"The convention committee would like to feature you both in a little friendly competition."

Her hand tightened on the sweaty glass. "Competition?" The word got stuck in her throat.

"Mr. Wallace actually made the suggestion. Based on his knowledge of the ground-breaking developments each of your companies has been making, he suggested that we give you a special opportunity to showcase your talent to the rest of the industry."

Liz's jaw dropped. "How does someone like Tyson Wallace know about our work? Or even know our names?"

With a friendly laugh, Laura patted her on the shoulder and said, "I have it on good authority that Tyson Wallace knows *everyone's* name and their business."

"What would the competition entail?"

"Oh, nothing too bloodthirsty, I assure you." She chuckled. "You'll both have a few added opportunities to showcase your work during the convention, including special pitch sessions for each of you. But you'll also have to get together to fill the empty lecture spot as a team, as well as prepare something special for the speech at the gala luncheon. I was a little worried about that part, I have to admit. But after seeing you here this evening and realizing that you already know each other, I have no doubt that you'll cooperate nicely."

Liz didn't know what to say.

"Before the end of the convention," Laura continued, "there'll be a vote of the attendees, and one of you will win the opportunity to meet with Mr. Wallace personally."

"Do you mean that he wants to see our portfolios?"

She lifted a hand. "As I'm sure you're already both aware, Tyson Wallace considers *one* new company per year to promote, based on innovation and value to the industry. The good news is that this year he's apparently already narrowed it down to one of the two of your companies. He's going to let the rest of us decide which one it will be."

The personal stamp of approval of Tyson Wallace would guarantee she'd be able to get the investment contribution she needed from Diego Vargas. How could he possibly resist investing then?

Ben hadn't said much, but he watched her, his gaze shuttered and heavy.

"What do you think?" she asked, biting her lip. It was quickly coming back to her, the familiar feeling of being in competition with Ben. Was he already planning how to steal the show and one-up her in order to get Tyson Wallace's attention? She wouldn't put it past him, especially after his year in New York. From what she'd read, he'd been an absolute shark, ruthless in doing anything it took to get his company off the ground, and she shuddered to think that he might have eventually stepped over her too, whether she'd agreed to work with him or not.

Not that she could blame him. A leopard doesn't change its spots, and she'd learned back in college just what kind of spots Ben had. He'd never hidden how driven he was to succeed. She considered herself just as driven—although maybe less manic about it—but they definitely had very different methods for achieving their goals. It wasn't that he was unethical in any way—just that he wouldn't think twice about taking the super hard-line approach to get what he wanted.

His expression never changed, but finally, he nodded.

"We'll do it," she said to Laura, projecting confidence and trying not to think about the many ways this could backfire if she wasn't careful.

"Good! I think this is going to be a wonderful inclusion in the program. I like the idea of bringing some new faces to the convention and encouraging a little bit of healthy competition. Maybe we'll make it an annual event!" She clapped her hands together and let out a happy sigh.

"We appreciate the opportunity," Liz said politely, feeling like a guinea pig. Ben nodded.

"It's my pleasure. Oh, and because you are both being so

wonderful about stepping up to the plate at the last minute like this, the committee would like to thank you with a surprise outing. Since you're here a little early I'm thinking it will work out nicely."

"What do you mean?"

"We've chartered a boat and hired a snorkeling instructor to take you both out for the day tomorrow. Doesn't that sound fun?"

Chapter Five

Liz awakened the next morning knowing that she'd dreamed of Ben Harrison. His business card was on her dresser. His scent was on the dress she'd draped over the chair before collapsing into bed last night. But more importantly, his image was burned into her brain. A hot flush was still all over her body, the tight edginess of need unfulfilled.

With a stretch, she fought the urge to turn over and pull the pillow over her head. Greeting the morning was like having an overly exuberant toddler you'd been cuddling with just a minute ago suddenly jumping up and down on the mattress beside you. She'd never liked getting up early, but she also hated wasting the day away, so she pulled herself out of bed and opened the heavy drapes to let in the beautiful morning sunshine.

It was late enough that she felt she could function, and she should be able to get some work done, even if she went out snorkeling with Ben later. She just hadn't quite decided if she was going to do that. It felt like a decidedly selfish and reckless thing to do.

The two of them on a boat together in the middle of the Atlantic wearing nothing but bathing suits?

No, she should use the time to get started on her presentations. Then again, she'd have to spend time with Ben to do that too, at least partly. And she *had* intended to have at least *one* day on the island for relaxation and fun.

Daniel was at the door as she was coming out of the shower.

"Hi, how was your night?" He asked her with a hug and a smile, brushing past her into the room with a paper bag in his hand. She'd expected him to harass her about Ben Harrison, but he actually looked cheerful.

"Good morning," she answered with a smile, happy to see him. "I have something to tell you."

He crossed the room and put the bag on her side table, then picked up the coffee pot from the little machine that had been provided for guest use. "Is it about you taking Tyson Wallace's spot as a presenter?" He asked, moving into the bathroom and filling the pot with water.

"How did you know about that?"

"The committee woman, Ms. Denham, called this morning. I think she had our room numbers mixed up."

"So, what do you think about their idea?" Liz bit her lip.

He came back into the room and stopped in front of her. There was a sparkle in his eyes and he grinned. "I think it's great. This is going to be huge for our visibility."

"You realize that we're sharing the spotlight with Ben Harrison, right?"

He shrugged. "Sure, but it's like you said last night.

We have confidence in our work and our vision, and we've busted our asses. Everyone else will have no choice but to see that, too. If we're ready, then we're ready."

"I agree," she said with a nod, a little surprised he was taking it so well after his tirade about Ben last night. "So we should get to work. We have to come up with some presentation ideas."

He picked up the bag and opened it up under her nose. She breathed in the delicious, fresh scent of croissants and groaned. "First thing's first," he said.

By the time she finished breakfast and coffee, Liz had convinced herself there wasn't time for the outing with Ben because they had too much work to do, but when he called up to say the car was waiting for them outside, Daniel wouldn't let her refuse and practically pushed her out the door. "Go on. I'll take care of everything here, and it'll give you a chance to share our presentation ideas with Harrison. Not to mention, if he's out with you, that's one less thing for me to worry about."

"What do you mean?"

He shook his head and thrust her beach bag into her arms. He turned her around and pushed her toward the door. "Nothing. Have a good time, today."

She gave him a look of warning over her shoulder. "Daniel."

"I'm serious. More and more conference attendees are arriving today, and if I'm going to start talking us up, it'll go better if Ben Harrison isn't around trying to muddy the waters. Besides, you deserve a break. If all goes well this morning, I may even take the afternoon off too. That *is* what we came here early for, isn't it?"

That was true, so she finally made her decision. She would throw caution to the wind for a few hours. "But I'll be back early," she promised. "In plenty of time to do some work."

Halfway to the lobby, she was already waffling, telling herself she could just go to the pool for the morning instead. But when the elevator door slid open and she saw Ben waiting for her across the hall, dressed in tan pants and a crisp white golf shirt, looking like he'd stepped right out of a magazine, she finally admitted she was excited to spend the day with him.

The heat must already be getting to her.

"Good morning." He smiled and stopped in front of her, his gaze travelling down the length of her in a quick, sharp slide.

There was certainly appreciation in that look, but there was also something more intense. She just couldn't quite figure out what it meant.

"You look great," he said. "Have you eaten yet? We could grab something on the way out." Had he doubted that she would show up? Well, then that made two of them.

"I had coffee and croissants in my room," she answered, and his palm went straight to the small of her back as they started walking, sliding against the smooth cotton of her sundress.

They passed the front desk to the hotel entrance where a porter was holding one of the large glass doors open for them.

"This is us." Ben pointed to a sparkling, clean, gun-metal gray Jeep waiting curbside in the circular driveway.

"Of course it is," she said with a wry smile. It was the kind of Jeep that had no roof and no doors, with big chunky wheels that would eat up any type of terrain. It was a total man car.

There was no one in the driver's seat. "I guess we have to wait for our guide."

Ben grinned and took her bag to toss it in the back. "Nope. You're looking at the guide."

She lifted her eyebrows and stared him down. "You? What's going on?"

"I talked to Laura this morning and told her we didn't need anyone."

"What? Why? Of course we need a guide."

"I know my way around the island well enough, so I thought it would be nice if it was just us today."

"You've been here before?" she asked with skepticism. "I find it hard to believe that you worked in some trips to Antigua as part of your world domination plan." From the first day they met, Ben had made it clear that he was focused on rising to the top as quickly and as completely as possible, starting with being top of the class.

He shrugged, but didn't say anything. She suddenly remembered that one of those pictures from the article in *Prestige* had been of him and the famous model Meredith Stone standing on the deck of a sleek motorboat.

"I ah…I'm not sure we should go out alone. What if something happens?"

He stepped closer and tipped her chin up. The sudden contact was startling, but not altogether unexpected. Ben had always been about making other people uncomfortable through confrontation, whereas she tended to avoid confrontation. She had no choice but to meet his gaze, and what she saw there made her pulse jump.

"I've missed you, Beth," he said. His earnest voice carved out a piece of her heart. "We used to spend whole days together."

"I remember," she whispered.

"So spend the day with me today. For old times' sake."

She shook her head and watched his shoulders tighten. He moved to turn away, but she grabbed his arm. "If I spend the day with you, it won't be for old times' sake," she said. "If we do this, it has nothing to do with the people we used to be. We live in the moment just for one day and don't think about yesterday…or tomorrow."

The heat in his eyes flared. "Deal."

She got in the Jeep and turned to look over her shoulder into the open rear seat. There was a large cooler back there, some snorkel equipment, and a navy blue duffel bag with "Optimus Inc." embroidered in yellow on the side of it.

She remembered when he had told her he was moving to New York and that he wanted her to go with him.

I've got a solid partnership offer in New York, and the industry there has started to really take off. If we stay in Seattle, we'd never get off the ground. The market here can't sustain another tech start-up, but in New York, we'd be unstoppable together.

I can't go to New York with you.

Why not? What's keeping you in Seattle?

He'd kissed her then. A kiss that still curled her toes when she dared think about it, that still woke her in the middle of the night with salty tears in her throat and his name on her lips. A kiss that had changed everything…*ruined* everything.

She'd shoved him away, her heart pounding so hard she hadn't known if it was out of exhilaration or abject fear.

What the hell did you do that for?

I've been wanting to do that for months.

Why? Why would you jeopardize what we have? Ruin our friendship?

We could be more than just friends, Beth. We could be more than just business partners too. All you have to do is take a leap of faith and come with me to New York. It'll be an adventure.

But Elizabeth Carlson was *not* the adventurous type, and she just couldn't do it. She couldn't take a leap of faith like that…not on a man like Ben.

She turned back around as he got in the car beside her and turned the ignition. "Do you know where you're going?" she asked as the engine revved, hoping her nervousness didn't show.

"Nope. But it's an island. How could we get lost?" His grin said he was having fun with her.

A smile pulled at her lips despite herself. She'd almost forgotten how easy it was to be around him, how quickly he could set her at ease, and how often he'd made her smile and laugh. "All you had to say was, 'yes, I know where we're going.'"

"But that isn't nearly as much fun as messing with you." He chuckled and snapped the gear shift into first.

She snorted and reached for her seat belt as he sped down the lane and through the tall iron gates of the resort. The wind whipped through the Jeep and tore at her hair. At first she tried to hold her sun hat on her head, but gave up soon enough and shoved it down on the floor between the seats in the back with everything else, even though it meant constantly tugging hair out of her mouth.

The Jeep accelerated, and she held tight to the little handlebar attached to the door. The roads were narrow and winding, but Ben drove with relaxed confidence. Her gaze fell to his fist on the ball of the gear shift. Veins popped under his skin and worked their way up his hand and arm. Hands like that could wreak havoc over her body.

She swallowed hard. Hands like that would be firm as they dragged over her skin. Firm and deliberate, knowing just where to put extra pressure, getting to know the feel and shape of her.

She shook herself and tried to find something else to focus on. The road they traveled wound away from the shoreline for a little while as they drove through a copse of trees. When it meandered back into the open, across the fields she caught random glimpses of the Caribbean, sparkling like jewels under the sun.

It was a little surreal being in such a place. It was even more surreal being here with Ben Harrison. She wasn't going to worry about it, though. Not now. It was a beautiful morning and promised to be a scorching hot day. She was in Antigua for goodness sake. It didn't matter who she was with or where they ended up, she was going to enjoy herself.

And that's an order.

With that decided, she burrowed into the narrow seat and sighed, letting all of her worries fall away…just for a little while.

She gazed out the window, amazed by the beauty of the island. As excited as she'd been coming off the airplane early yesterday morning, it had been a long, overnight flight from Seattle with a delayed stop in Miami. She'd wanted to pay attention to the sights on the drive from the airport, but nodding in and out in the taxi had been more her speed by that point, so this was her first good look at everything.

"The resort we're staying at is close to the English Harbour, which is nice and deep and has some good diving areas," Ben said, raising his voice to be heard over the air rushing between them. "But I wanted to take you to Cades Reef. It's beautiful there. The snorkeling is great, and part of the reef has been turned into an underwater reserve. That's where the boat is waiting for us."

She'd never been on a boat, at least not a real one with an actual motor. Hell, she'd never been snorkeling before either. It was starting to sound like she was in over her head before she'd even gotten into the water.

"Are you okay with this?" He frowned, no doubt reading her silence as insecurity. "If you're not comfortable with it, we could always turn around and hang out back at the resort, or just go to the beach for the day."

"No," she croaked with a wave of her hand. "You were right, this sounds like it will be loads of fun. I love to snorkel." Turning away so he couldn't see her grimace, she focused on the dirt road winding out in front of the Jeep.

Why couldn't she just tell him she barely knew how to swim, and snorkeling sounded like something you did in front of the bathroom mirror with a mouth full of Listerine?

Growing up two hours from the Pacific coast meant nothing when she'd rarely gotten out of the city because normal family excursions would have meant time away from work, and neither of her parents had ever heard of the word "vacation."

When her mother died from cancer—which might have been caught earlier if she hadn't stubbornly refused to take time off from work to see a doctor—her father had actually given it a half-assed shot. He took a single day off work during the height of the summer when she was seventeen and Daniel was thirteen, rented a rickety old tin boat with wooden oars, and brought them fishing for the afternoon.

That trip was the only memory she had of her father that didn't involve a glowing computer screen between them or the interruption of an important conference call. Even so, the memory had always tasted bittersweet, probably because it was all she had. And even that had been too little, too late. Liz's father died in a car crash the following spring, without even seeing her graduate from high school. Not that he would have been there if he'd lived…it probably would have conflicted with a business meeting.

Neither of their parents had ever noticed how their intense career focus had alienated them from their children—and even each other, since she couldn't remember seeing them connect on a personal level in any meaningful way. But it turned out there wouldn't have been enough time for either of them to change their ways even if they'd wanted to. They both died too soon…no doubt thinking at the very end that their biggest regret would be leaving their work unfinished.

She pinched her eyes closed against the rush of bitterness she hadn't allowed herself to feel in years, and started to tell Ben she had no idea how to snorkel. But her jaw snapped shut again before even a squeak came out. Stubborn, stubborn.

She'd rather drown in a dramatic tangle of flailing arms and flippered legs than declare out loud that she couldn't keep up with this particular man on a simple vacation outing. And if that made her bull-headed, then so be it.

She turned her attention back to the scenery. Pretty soon

she was entranced, soaking in the sunshine and marvelling at the colorful plant life. Beyond the road and the hills, she could see the clear blue-green of the sea, and a ton of sailing ships out in the harbor spreading their sails. One of them in particular was huge. It would take a pirate crew to sail that thing. She hoped to God that wasn't the kind of "boat" Ben had been talking about.

After a few minutes of silence, she caught him watching her. "Are you having a good time?" he asked.

"How could I not? This place is gorgeous." She grinned and threw up her hands, feeling amazingly free. The wind was warm on her face, the scenery was breathtaking, and Ben was looking at her like she was the only woman in the world. She could handle this. In fact, she never wanted it to end.

Ben stepped on the gas, and she squealed as they took the next turn, slapping her hands on whatever she could grab—which happened to be his thigh. She quickly pulled back and gave him a dirty look, but he only laughed.

They drove by another small field. "Oh wait, look at that. Slow down." She pointed, glancing over at him in her excitement. "Look at those tall white birds standing next to the cows. I'm surprised they don't get trampled."

"Those are cattle birds, a type of egret. You'll only find one bird standing guard for each cow. They wait there for the animal's hooves to stir the ground and then snatch up the juicy insects that surface from the disturbed earth."

The entire drive was amazing. She was soon pointing to everything from coconut and cinnamon trees to pelicans and green lizards. Ben would tell her about them all, sounding as knowledgeable as any one of the locals. It was like having her very own tour guide, and she couldn't hold in her enthusiasm and wonder.

"How do you know all this stuff?"

"You know me," he said with a shrug, turning back to face the road. "I don't go into any situation without knowing everything I can about it. Whether it's my surroundings or…" he glanced at her sharply. "…my competition."

That was the first time he'd mentioned their businesses. She swallowed hard. "So, am I your competition?"

"It would seem so, wouldn't it?"

She nodded.

He sighed. "It didn't have to be that way. We could have been working together."

"Don't." She stopped him, not ready for this conversation. "It wasn't right. We would have been horrible business partners, and I could never have left Seattle."

Surprisingly, he let it go. When she glanced back at him, his face was a mask of thoughtfulness.

A little while later, they parked the Jeep and walked down the boardwalk to the docks. She followed him, but wasn't paying much attention to where they were going, because she was staring at all the yachts. When Ben stopped and pointed to the boat they were going to take to the reef, her mouth fell open in shock and dismay. "That isn't a boat. It's a race car on water."

The monstrosity had to be at least thirty-five feet long. Not as big as most of the other boats, but too big for a simple snorkeling trip for two people. It looked like a shark coming out of the water, all pointy up at the front like a fin—was the front called the bow? Or was it the aft? The stern? Beth knew as much about boats as a cat did about cross-stitch.

Either way, what she could only assume was the hood of the boat extended across the top to a windshield at about the half-way point, which came over the dash and front driver and passenger seats. Then the rest of the deck was left open to the balmy sea air.

Maybe it was shaped like that for aerodynamics. That, and the two propeller things sitting in the water on the back of the boat probably meant it went really fast.

Like…super fast.

Her heart did a quick double thump.

Speaking of fast, the paint job was all white and black stripes that ended in a decorative, sporty swirl. The boat had dark tinted windows like the rebuilt Mustang her high school boyfriend used to drive around town. She'd broken up with him after he drag raced some other guy in a souped-up Honda Civic on the curving mountain roads, with her in the passenger seat.

A railing went all the way around the front of the boat—she was pretty sure boat people called it the bow—of the ship. *Ship. Not a boat.* It didn't feel right to call this a simple boat.

"Where's the captain?"

He smiled. "I'm the captain."

"Somehow, I can't believe the hotel or the tour company or whoever owns this thing is okay with letting us take that out all by ourselves. Wouldn't we need some kind of license?"

"I mentioned that I've been to Antigua before, right? I guess I forgot to add that I have a boating license." Ben threw the snorkel gear over the little railing.

He held out his hand with a raised brow. "Are you okay with this? I just figured that this way we'll be able to spend as much time out on the water as we want, and there'll be no one else around to get in the way."

"It seems to me that's something you could have mentioned back at the hotel before we left."

"You were already on the verge of cancelling. That would have pushed you over the edge."

She sputtered. "You don't know that."

"And you need this break," he continued.

"You're starting to sound like my friend Sarah."

"Are you saying you weren't *this close* to coming up with an excuse not to come today?"

He was right, and they both knew it. She glared up at him, but after a long moment she muttered a choice swear word under her breath, grabbed his hand, and let him lead her up onto the deck.

The idea of willingly letting him drive her around in this speeding, sinkable death trap made her break out in hives, but she was determined never to admit it and get the whole thing over with as quickly as possible.

That didn't mean the ship wasn't absolutely gorgeous. The deck was made of beautifully polished cedar, and the chairs and benches spread out across the back end were upholstered in a pristine white leather. Sitting out in the open with all the gulls flying overhead, it was like begging one of them to drop a present, but she supposed not even the birds dared mar the perfection of the water craft.

She looked around at all the spotless chrome and the pristine, polished wood floors. The hatch leading down into the hull of the boat was open, and she caught a glimpse of mirrors and more leather. It didn't look very big, but had they managed to fit a bed down there?

Never mind. She didn't want to know that.

"What do you want me to do?" She was completely out of her element and was pretty sure it showed.

"You don't need to do a thing. Just sit down and relax while I get us launched."

"Okay."

"Do you have a cell phone or any other valuables that you want me to store? Wouldn't want anything to get wet that shouldn't get wet."

She shook her head. "I didn't bring anything."

There was a long bench seat at the back of the boat behind the captain's chair, and she perched on it stiffly while Ben put his cell phone in the boat's dashboard compartment and then went to store their gear below deck. When he returned, he handed her a bottle of water and took a long swig from another one, head tipped back. A single drop escaped his lips, tracking down his chin and the column of his throat. She held her breath and followed its progress into the collar of his shirt.

She snapped the cap on her bottle and took a small, distracted sip, watching him over the small circular rim. The water was nice and cold, a good check on her overheated libido, which was obviously flaring up at the slightest provocation.

He strolled about the deck taking stock. After only a minute or two, Liz heard his cell phone ring from within the dash. He glanced over but didn't rush to answer it. "Shouldn't you get that?" she asked, remembering how her father could never let the phone ring more than once before he grabbed it.

"It's fine, everyone knows I've got the day off today."

She raised her eyebrows, but hid a smile behind her water

bottle. She noted the way his biceps flexed as he unsnapped covers and wrapped them up for storage. He disembarked to do a walkabout of the craft, smiling at people hanging out on the dock as he did whatever it was he needed to do to get ready for them to leave.

She found herself twisting around to keep him in her sights, even leaning her chin on her arms to watch him move. Then he came back on board and started flipping switches on instrument panels. Hell, even the way he did *that* was sexy. *Damn it*.

Her mouth went dry when he bent over the edge of the boat to catch the ropes someone down on the dock had untied and threw up to him.

Ben moved to stand in front of the wheel—which was no bigger than one you would see in a car and didn't look anything like the big captain's wheels on the pirate ships in the movies.

When he started the engine, it roared to life before settling down to a gentle purr. Her fingers clenched on the seat cushion in a death grip, but she had to trust that he actually did know what he was doing.

At least it certainly looked as if he'd done this before.

He turned to her and grinned. Dark sunglasses perched on top of his head, and he dropped them down to cover his eyes. Her chest tightened, but she couldn't look away, and soon she was smiling back at him, still surprised by the revelation that he'd been to Antigua before and had his own boating license. It didn't match the driven, single-minded man she remembered.

His hair had been tossed around a bit by the breeze. He looked wicked and carefree, like a young Indiana Jones on the first step of a new adventure—without the wide-brimmed hat. "Are you ready?" he asked over the rumble of the engine.

There was no turning back. She gave him a thumbs up, hoping like hell she wasn't prone to seasickness.

...

Ben slowly pulled away from the dock and navigated the harbor carefully, mindful of the crowded slips and the shore snorkelers hanging around in the shallows.

Cades Reef wasn't too far out, and it was a beautiful, calm day on the water, so he was optimistic that underwater visibility would be good. If he'd wanted to really show Beth something spectacular, there were better, more challenging places to snorkel in and around the island, but even though she hadn't come right out and admitted it, he was almost positive she hadn't done anything like this before, and he didn't want to push her too hard, too fast.

He could have left everything alone and let the guide take them out snorkeling as planned, but seeing Beth again had made him realize just how much he'd missed the combustive chemistry between them. Today was an opportunity to seize the moment and let that chemistry finally work for him—so he could purge her persistent memory once and for all.

He tipped his face to the hot sun and let it warm him all the way through as he navigated the boat between the tall, colored buoys marking the harbor's exit. He was excited to show Beth the reef and knew that he wouldn't have felt the same way with just anyone.

He used to love a good challenge, but that spark had been

missing since the devastating circumstances surrounding his would-be-partner Jeffrey Olsen's death. He'd snuffed it out on purpose, but now he was kind of glad to get it back again, because he knew he would never make the same mistakes. He would be careful and more aware of those around him.

"You do that pretty well for a guy who supposedly spent the last year getting a new business up and running," Beth called out to him, her hand over her eyes against the beaming sun as she watched.

"I'm a man of many talents." He threw her an unrepentant grin and noticed she'd put that big floppy hat back on. A gust of wind blew up off the water and threatened to take the hat. She scrambled to grab it before it could blow away. He liked the way she stubbornly smashed it back onto her head. It was absolutely adorable.

When was the last time he had thought of anything as *adorable*?

"And you make it look easy. You always made everything look easy." She shifted in her seat, re-crossing her long legs, and hell, but he liked that too.

"Starting a business is definitely a lot harder than college ever was," he admitted. "If I didn't have a friend who insisted on dragging me out here every once in a while in an attempt to make me relax, I probably wouldn't even know what sunshine looks like."

"Meredith Stone?" she asked. Was that jealousy in her voice or just wishful thinking on his part? "I saw the pictures of you and her. Isn't she a lingerie model or something?"

He smiled. *Definitely jealous*. "Meredith doesn't model anymore. Now she designs and sells her own brand of lingerie."

"She sounds very...accomplished. How did you meet

her?"

"We met through my business partner, Steve Nolan."

"She's a beautiful woman."

"Yes." Maybe he should tell her about his relationship with Meredith, but it was complicated, and he refused to ruin the mood. It was too fragile and hard-won to risk.

Beth's brows lifted in a delicate arch of skepticism. He even liked that, too. He liked everything about her. Maybe he should tell her *that*, but the time wasn't right yet. He was pretty sure the cautious, reserved woman he'd known a year ago was still somewhere inside this confident, sexy siren. If he admitted how crazy she made him feel, she'd back away quicker than a skittish kitten. He'd spook her…like he spooked her before he went to New York.

He wanted her to admit that they could never have stayed just friends. What they'd felt for one another was too strong. They would have had to confront it sooner or later, whether he'd pressed the issue or not.

She looked out across the water, so he didn't pursue it. He hadn't intended for today to be about the past, anyway. He wanted both of them to have a good time, so instead, he faced forward and pointed. They'd just cleared the harbor, were now coasting in the slightly deeper water that opened up into the sea, but he could still make out the coral shelf.

"That's Cades Reef."

"It's so beautiful." Her voice was high with wonder. It was infectious, almost as if he could keep a piece of her joy for himself just by standing close to her.

Beth had scooted closer to the side and was looking over the boat carefully as if she was afraid it would tip if she got too close to the edge. The water here still wasn't much more than ten feet deep, but it was so clear you could see right to the bottom.

She laughed and pointed at a sea turtle, darting out from beneath the hull of the boat toward a large section of brightly colored coral.

He had an idea. Lifting his arm, he motioned for her to come to him. "Are you ready?"

His gaze wandered the length of her again, appreciating the rise of her breasts, the curve of her waist…and those drop-dead gorgeous legs.

Suddenly, the question had a double meaning he hadn't quite intended.

"Ready for what?" She eyed his outstretched hand with a suspicious glint in her eyes before glancing out over the twinkling blue ripples in the sea as if she was worried they would turn into monstrous waves and swallow the boat whole.

"You aren't nervous, are you?" he teased.

She lifted her chin and glared at him. "What do I have to be nervous about?"

He shook his head. "Not a thing, the boat is perfectly safe." She took that bottom lip back between her teeth again. This was a new habit of hers that he'd noticed last night, but holy hell it was one he could get used to. He imagined himself pulling her plump lip with his teeth, and when she groaned at the sharp pain, licking it.

Jesus. If he didn't control himself, he was going to make a mess of things.

"I was thinking of taking a bit of a detour on the way to our snorkeling site. What do you say? Do you want to drive? Why don't we open her up and see how fast this machine can go?"

She jerked her head up in surprise. "Oh no. We don't have to do that. I mean, I don't have a license or anything."

"I'll be right here the whole time."

"What if I break it? This thing has got to be more expensive than my car."

"Come on." He knew exactly how to get the reaction he was looking for. "Don't tell me you're…"

...

"Don't say it!"

"*Chicken*." He actually said it. The jerk. She gritted her teeth and crossed her arms.

"You know you want to, Beth."

She narrowed her gaze in response to his taunting.

"It's not that hard. I mean, if I can do it, then surely you—"

She jumped to her feet and whipped off her sunhat, shoving it into his chest. She ignored the grin on his face and the thumping of her heart as she stepped up and edged her way into position in front of the wheel. She could do this.

Out of the corner of her eye, she watched him toss her hat away. It sailed across the deck like a Frisbee. "That's better," he murmured into her ear a moment later.

She was surprised to find him so close behind her and froze, holding her breath.

"You okay?" he asked.

She didn't want to miss anything and accidentally push the one button that would sink the boat. She nodded, deliberately putting aside her awareness of him so she could focus on his instructions. But that was easier said than done.

He turned off the ignition with a twist of the key. "I'll show you how all the instruments work, and then you can give it a shot. It really isn't hard to learn at all."

When his arms came around her and settled on the wheel, she drew in a sharp breath. She forced herself to stay relaxed—or at least appear to be relaxed. There was no reason why she should read anything into his proximity. He wasn't even touching her.

…And then he was.

His chest pressed up against her shoulder blades, and his cheek was right next to hers as he leaned forward and flipped a switch. Whatever aftershave he'd used was unfamiliar, but it smelled amazing, like sandalwood and amber.

When he spoke, she got shivers all the way to her toes. "This is the power. Like a car, the boat has a battery for all the electrical systems, as well as fuel to run the engine. Once the key is in the ignition like this, you need to flick on the power." He flicked the switch back up again and she watched all the dials jump to attention, much like the tiny hairs on the back of her neck as his words caressed her cheek softly.

"We need power," she croaked, trying to ignore the fluttering of her stomach. "Got it."

"Then you're going to check all the gauges and make sure the systems are in order." He tapped a glass-covered window. "This is the gas gauge. And this one here is the speedometer."

"Okay. And what about that?" She pointed to another display.

As he explained what everything meant, his hand went to her hip, resting there like it was the most natural thing in the world for him to do. It was almost impossible for her to concentrate, but she knew if she didn't focus she would embarrass herself when the time came to take the wheel of this thing. That, or she would embarrass herself by spinning around and demanding to be kissed.

"Um, so what is this for?" She gripped the handle to her right.

"That's the throttle. It's basically like the clutch of a car." He put his hand over top of hers and squeezed. The firm touch felt more intimate than he doubtless intended it to be. She hoped he couldn't feel the mad gallop of her racing heart.

"Before you start the engine, you've got to prime it, like this." His thumb pressed a button on the side edge of the throttle handle, and he started throwing it forward and back. He did it three times, her hand still trapped beneath his. "You keep your finger on this button and *pump* the throttle." He cleared his throat. "Forward and back. Just a few times, there you go. Pump it."

His voice had lowered, grown huskier. With one hand guiding hers, the other slid over the soft cotton of her sundress as he opened his palm over her belly. She tensed as waves of heat spread outward in a circle from the center of her.

Suddenly, all she really wanted was to leave this thing in park right here in the middle of the open water and have those hands working their way over every inch of her naked body. She wanted to feel the heat of the sun on her face and the heat of his touch everywhere else.

But that would be giving in…so easily. She couldn't make it so easy on him…could she?

With a hitch in her breath, she tilted her chin to look

up at him. The burning flames in his eyes scorched her. His mouth was so close, so tempting. As she watched, he pressed his lips together into a thin line as if he was also holding himself back by a thin thread of control.

At least she wasn't the only one who appeared to be getting inappropriately turned on by a simple lesson in the operation of a motorboat.

"What do I do next?" she whispered, her gaze still locked with his. Feeling emboldened, she leaned back just a fraction of an inch.

An inch was all that had been separating them, and now the whole hard length of him was pressed deliciously against her. From her thighs to her shoulders, she felt him there, not quite demanding, but insistent. Not unyielding, but solid and real.

He didn't take advantage of her movement to come even closer. Instead, he cleared his throat. "Let's get the motor started."

She stifled a groan and turned her attention forward. After a weighted pause, Ben knocked the handle back into the upward locked position. "Go ahead and turn the ignition."

With shaking fingers and her head full of everything but driving the boat, Liz reached out and turned the key, bringing the engine to powerful, roaring life. It rumbled beneath her feet, in the floorboards, and all around them. Two of the dials in the dash behind the wheel jumped up again, fluttering a little bit before the engine settled into a deep, restful purr.

Her other hand was still under Ben's on the handle of the throttle. Pressing the button once more to release it, he let go again quickly, and when he shoved the throttle forward, he did it slowly. It moved smoothly, and she could feel the power of the engine behind it.

The boat started to inch forward. Ben edged back again, letting go of her hand and holding onto the side of the boat instead. He planted his feet farther apart behind her, like a real sailor bracing himself for the rolling waves on the deck of a ship, and so she did the same. *It really does make you feel a little more stable.*

"There you go," he said. "Now, the more you push the throttle that way, the faster we'll go. When you want to slow down again just pull it back, but try and keep your movements smooth and—"

He broke off as the vehicle jerked forward. She'd incorrectly estimated the amount of pressure she would need against the handle of the throttle and shoved it down way too hard.

The nose of the boat reared up into the air like a breaching whale coming up out of the water, and then the craft jumped ahead. She pitched forward violently, smashing her knee on the console in front of her. She pictured those two large propeller things at the back of the boat digging beneath the surface, churning the water into an angry white foam, but didn't dare look back.

Ben's arm came around her waist just as she would have hit her head on the windshield. He jerked her back into direct, undeniable contact within the protection of his hard body.

The nose of the boat evened out slowly as they picked up speed, and in the blink of an eye, they were *flying* across the water so fast she couldn't catch her breath.

She squeaked and yanked her hand off the throttle, and

Ben immediately reached for it, pulling the throttle back in a smooth, controlled motion. As the boat slowed and then stopped, he returned it to the locked position.

The boat rocked forward and back and even side to side. This was no gentle, floating movement with the sea. They had disturbed the water, and the sea was rebelling against them. Waves slammed up against the hull and splashed right into the boat, pouring over her toes and calves, leaving the hem of her sundress clinging to her thighs, and soaking the cuffs of Ben's pants.

"Smooth, slow movements," he repeated with a chuckle. The arm around her waist squeezed.

"Oh my God. I almost killed us."

"No you didn't. Don't worry." He briskly rubbed her arms. "It would have taken a lot more than that to flip us, and trust me, this thing is harder to sink than it looks. Let's try it again, but this time we'll just go a little slower."

She almost said no, but she couldn't give up just yet. After taking a deep breath, she reached forward and put her hand on the throttle. She depressed the button, then *carefully* started to push the handle forward.

This time the boat gradually began to move through the water, picking up speed like a reasonably accelerating car.

"There, that's better," he said. She could hear the smile in his voice as he stayed in place behind her. "See how it feels?"

She nodded and glanced forward. Her breathing hitched. "We're listing to the left a little, aren't we?"

His arms came around her again. This time he rested those big hands on the wheel, enveloping her with warmth and strength. "So steer the boat where you want it to go," he said.

After a few more minutes, her heartbeat calmed down, and she relaxed a little bit. With her hands on the wheel, she took in the vastness of the beautiful sea spread out ahead of them.

With the shore of Antigua at their backs, it was like looking at the end of the world, cloudless blue sky meeting calm blue water, with a couple of little islands here and there to break it up. She even steered the boat around one of them. It was barely big enough to be home to the trio of trees growing in the middle of it.

Ben had stepped back to give her more space. She slowly turned and saw him sitting back with his arms spread out across the bench seat and one foot propped up on his knee. He watched her with a shuttered expression that was serious, thoughtful, and a little dangerous, all at the same time, and she quickly faced forward again.

"You're doing great, Beth."

She glanced back over her shoulder. The serious look had smoothed out like it had never been there, and he was grinning. "Are you ready to open her up and go a bit faster?"

She laughed. "No, I think I've satisfied my curiosity. Why don't you take over? I'll just lay back and soak in the sunshine for a while now."

When he came up behind her, she let go of the wheel and retreated to a safe distance, pushing her thick, curly hair back behind her ears before swiping her hands over her hips and thighs, smoothing out the invisible wrinkles in her dress.

"Why don't we head to the reef and do some snorkeling?" he suggested, reminding her that had been the plan all along.

She arranged the damp fabric of her skirt around her

knees before clasping her hands in her lap. The morning had advanced nicely, and the sky was a clear stunning blue, the sun bright and hot. The heat would continue to mount as the day wore on. Up on deck there was virtually no escaping it, but she loved it.

She pretended not to notice the way Ben continued to watch her, but it was impossible to ignore the weight of his regard. Her nipples tightened beneath the thin protection of her clothing.

The silence only made it worse, so she rushed to fill it. "So, has New York been everything you hoped it would be?"

He gazed out over the water, then down at the gadget displays on the dash. "Yes and no. I'd never been anywhere other than Seattle my whole life. I thought I was prepared, but I guess I wasn't."

Something in his voice made her think there was more to it than that. "Did something happen?"

When he looked back at her, there was a tightness in his expression, and she almost felt guilty for asking.

"I killed a man," he said.

Chapter Six

"*What?*"

He winced, wondering how much to say, deciding it wasn't worth keeping anything back. "When I left Seattle to partner with Jeffrey Olsen, I thought it was going to be the beginning of something great, and on paper it should have been. Olsen had distribution connections that I didn't have, but he'd been having trouble mastering the tech, and I already had a patent. We were each going to bring something equally important to the table."

"Olsen," she said with a frown. "Jeffrey Olsen? Where have I heard that name recently?"

"Maybe from the news reports when he died a few months ago?"

She nodded. "Yes, that's it. But I read that he killed himself because his company went bankrupt."

"He killed himself when I backed out of our business deal."

She gasped, clearly shocked—exactly the response he expected should anyone else discover just how close the timing had been between the fallout of their business partnership and Olsen's death.

"Why would you back out?" she asked.

"Almost from day one, he started making bad business decisions, and he refused to listen to me when I told him we needed to try something different. He said that he was more experienced, and I should be grateful that he had decided to take me under his wing."

She groaned and put a hand on her hip. "I think I know exactly how well that would have gone over."

He nodded. "So I walked."

"But why would Olsen kill himself?"

"When I left, a few of his people came with me. They all smelled the blood in the water. I had been his last chance. He'd done his best to hide it until he could lock me into a partnership agreement, but it didn't work. He needed me more than I needed him, and when our agreement fell apart, he couldn't make another deal to save his life." Poor choice of words.

"But you didn't actually kill him."

He swallowed hard. "I didn't give a shit about Olsen," he admitted. "When I realized I had come all the way to New York only to get jerked around, I cut him loose without a second thought. It was cutthroat and callous."

"But you didn't know he was going to kill himself."

"No, but I knew he was desperate." He shrugged off the past, even though he felt anything but casual about it. "If the media had gotten wind of the events leading up to his death, who knows how they would have spun my involvement in the whole mess."

Thankfully, she didn't ask him any more questions for a while.

He maneuvered the boat nice and easy, generating very little wake as they knifed through the water. Every once in a while he pointed something out for her, enjoying her excitement in the discovery. A line of mangrove trees along the shore. An interesting fish here, and some coral there.

They approached a section of reef. The area had gotten busy, but the tour boats had spread themselves out for privacy. Ben picked a secluded spot in deeper water just beyond the shelf, and pulled the boat to a stop. "We'll have to leave the boat out a little bit because the reef gets too shallow, and we don't want to damage the ecosystem with our prop. If we stay here, we'll still be able to swim to the shelf and hopefully see quite a bit of marine life," he said. "Take the wheel for me while I grab the anchor."

This time she walked up to the wheel without a twitch of the nervousness he'd seen in her earlier, making his chest swell with pride for her bravery. "What do you need me to do?" she asked.

"If we start drifting too much before I've had a chance to drop the anchor, you can use this lever." He pointed. "It's kind of like a joystick that controls the inboard trolling motor. But this motor has a much smaller prop on the end of it, with just enough power to keep us stable until I've got the boat tied up tight."

She nodded and came up beside him, her shoulder brushing his arm so that he almost changed his mind about stepping away. But if he didn't, they were definitely going to start to drift…and not just on the water.

He lifted one of the seat covers and pulled out a large anchor on a heavy chain attached to a thick black rope. He braced one knee on the bench and held the hunk of iron over the edge of the boat and slowly lowered it into the water before tying it off on a hook attached to the hull.

After going down to change into his swim trunks, Ben returned on deck with a towel over his shoulders to the most arresting sight anywhere on land or sea.

The neckline of Beth's sundress gaped open almost to her waist. She glanced up and saw him standing there, and they both froze. Her eyes widened as she looked him up and down. In that moment he was certain of at least one thing—Beth liked what she saw from her vantage point as much as he did from his. The heat of her awareness sprang up between them, and it made every muscle in his body taut and ready.

She shrugged the printed dress off her shoulders and let it fall down her arms. The whole thing fluttered down her body and pooled on the deck at her feet.

"Damn." He let out a long whistle of appreciation. "Are you sure you want to go snorkeling?"

She grinned. With a playful shrug, she bent down for her dress and pretended to put it back on. "You mean you want to go back to the hotel and work instead?"

He groaned. "I'll get the snorkeling gear."

Determined to cool off, he did exactly that while Beth laughed and folded her dress into her beach bag. She had pulled out a bottle of sunscreen and was applying it to her arms and chest when he returned. "Here, let me help you with that." He wasn't about to pass up the chance to run his hands over her smooth, creamy skin.

She sent him a raised brow, but he dropped the snorkeling gear on the bench beside them and took the bottle from her hand.

Heat. Sticky and moist. The air crackled with it until she finally twisted around to give him her back. He tightened his stomach muscles and took a deep breath before squeezing a dollop of sunscreen into his palm, rubbing his hands together, and then laying them on her arms.

...

Ben smoothed the sunscreen into her skin. He started by kneading her shoulders. The mini-massage felt amazing. Some of the tension that had been sitting there for too long was soothed, although another sort of tension only got worse.

As his touch burned over every inch of her back—even under the straps of her bikini top so that nothing was missed—it was easy to imagine that there *was* no bikini.

Her breathing grew shallow and fast. His hands went lower, smoothing down the line of her spine to her tailbone before moving over her hips.

He spread his fingers and slipped them into her bottoms, caressing the top of her butt. She shuddered and took a few steps forward until his hands fell away. "I, ah…I think I can do the rest. Thanks." Her cheeks were warm and her nipples tight as she hurriedly did her arms and legs.

Finally, she squared her shoulders and spun around with a smile. "So, are we going to do this thing or not?"

Ben handed her the flippers and goggles, and when she just looked at them hanging from her fingers, he grinned.

"Now would be a good time to fess up that you've never been snorkeling before."

She looked down at the water. "It's that obvious, is it?"

He laughed and showed her how to put the flippers on, but the touch of his hands on her ankles and calves was just another distraction. When she stood up and pulled the mask over her head, it snagged in her hair, and he helped her fix it, smiling into her eyes until she blushed. His fingers barely touched the side of her face, but it was enough to make her pulse leap.

He stepped back and put his hands on his hips and surveyed his handiwork. "There. You look like a natural."

She chuckled. "Until I get in the water and start flailing about."

"You know how to swim. I remember that much."

"Yep, but I assume this is a little different than doing laps in the pool at the student athletic facility."

"It'll be easy. And I'll be right there with you," he assured her.

He jumped in the water like it was nothing, coming right back up to the surface to wait for her. He shook his head and pulled on the goggles, gently treading water. She thought about climbing safely down the ladder that folded out off the back of the boat, but he looked up with a grin, and she knew she had to jump, too.

She sputtered and coughed coming back up, but had to admit the water was amazing. Refreshing but not cold, and so clear she could see…everything.

Breathing only through her mouth was distracting at first. It took all of her concentration, and she couldn't focus on all the sights. But then there was a moment when she just seemed to get it. She fell into a rhythm of breathing and realized it wasn't as bad as she'd thought it would be.

In fact, snorkeling was fun. She floated on top of the water, relaxed as could be, watching a completely different world below the surface. The reef teemed with life. Colorful and vibrant. She didn't want to touch anything, afraid of sending all the fish into hiding.

Ben had no such fears. He swam up beside her, eyes magnified behind the face mask, and took the snorkel out of his mouth. He pointed to her and put his hand over his mouth, and she understood that he was telling her to take out the snorkel, too, and hold her breath.

She nodded, and he took her hand and pulled her deeper, closer to the coral for a good look.

They came up to the surface, and Liz took long, deep breaths, scissoring her legs to tread water. "That's the most amazing and beautiful thing I've ever experienced." She shoved her facemask up over her forehead. She couldn't keep the massive grin off her face. "I feel like I'm on the Discovery Channel."

"Not quite the most beautiful thing I've seen today," Ben said with a pointed look into her eyes. "But I definitely wouldn't have missed it."

His regard felt weighty and intense, and she found herself floating closer until the soft waves coming across the water's surface broke against the two of them as one. She looked up, wondering if he might finally kiss her, hoping he might finally kiss her.

Tingles of anticipation exploded over her skin when his hand touched her shoulder and smoothed all the way to her elbow.

He leaned in, his mouth close to the curve of her jaw. She held her breath.

"Look at that," he whispered.

That wasn't what she'd been expecting. He turned her around, pressed his chest up against her back, and pointed. She gasped, but not because of the turtle that was swimming in the water a short distance away.

"Is that a sea turtle?" she asked. "It's huge."

"Yes." His face was next to hers, over her shoulder. "I've never seen one. This is a first for me too."

She looked up. "I'm glad we shared something that is new to both of us today."

Something passed between them that felt more intimate than she was prepared for, maybe more intimate than he was prepared for, too. He cleared his throat and gently floated back a bit.

"Come on," he said in a cheerful voice. "Let's see what else we can find."

The two of them explored for hours, coming up for air and going back down, then swimming near the surface again so they could rest and breathe through their snorkels. Every time she thought about telling him they should call it a day and start to head back, she changed her mind because she wasn't ready for the experience to end. When guilt threatened, she choked it down. There would be more than enough time for work later.

When a moray eel passed in front of her, she was amazed that it looked like it was *slithering* through the water, and she motioned excitedly for Ben to come see it, too. He reminded her not to touch with a shake of his head, and they watched from a safe distance as it disappeared back into the coral.

Ben pointed out sea grasses, lots of different kinds of fish, and at least four different types of coral. He grinned when she reached out to touch a flowerpot coral, and it pulled back in on itself like a curling fern leaf.

During it all, he took more and more opportunities to touch her. His hands spanned her bare waist as they came up for air, and he caressed her shoulder to get her attention. As they swam, his body constantly brushed against hers, making her very aware of the shape and size of him. The way he cut through the water mesmerized her, his muscles sleek and defined. He swam as if it was second nature, and part of her was jealous. The other part of her just thrilled to watch him.

All in all, it was one of the most amazing afternoons she'd ever experienced, but finally, despite wanting to see everything, every nook and cranny of the reef, she was getting tired. Her fingers were pruney, and despite herself, thoughts of what needed to be done in preparation for the convention were starting to creep back into the forefront of her mind.

They were a few feet beneath the surface, and she tugged on Ben's arm, motioning toward the boat. He nodded and pointed for her to go on ahead, he would follow right behind.

The deep hull of the boat dug into the water about six or seven hundred feet away, the stainless steel ladder hanging off the back, catching the sun with a bit of a flash. She started to rise to the surface to blow out her snorkel and get some air to make the swim back.

Something brushed against her flank. At first she thought it was Ben swimming up beside her, but it hadn't felt like Ben. Maybe a fish. But it was sharp and quick, like sand paper scratching across her skin. She swiped at her hip and saw the long, muscular gray body arching away from her and descending back down below.

A fin. A triangular tail.

Shark.

Her panic was immediate. She stopped swimming and started choking.

The snorkel hung from its clip on her goggles, banging her in the chin. Even if she had been wearing it, she didn't think she would have been able to breathe through the thing if her life depended on it.

She flailed and kicked her legs, twisting around and looking back and forth.

Where did it go?

If she hadn't been submerged in water, she'd be sweating bullets. The shark had disappeared, and suddenly the sea was cold, her blood like ice in her veins.

Ben grabbed her arm, and she let out a little scream, taking in water.

Choking, choking. Oh my God, can't breathe. Get me up. Get me out of here.

Her lungs burned. *Up and out, need to get out.* She couldn't see the shark, needed to get to the surface right away.

Both of Ben's arms went around her, and he held her still. His flippered legs kicked in a smooth, controlled pace. Would that attract the shark? Her eyes widened as she struggled to see around him, but he shook his head, tilting her chin up until she looked at him. Her lungs burned, her chest felt too tight. Was she going to drown here before the shark could even take its first bite?

His calm reached out for her, catching and holding her gaze. She forced herself to take a mental pause and nodded, but her lungs were burning for air.

Finally he pointed up toward the surface. They were almost there. She blinked and nodded, but when she would have darted the rest of the way, he held her back and made her go slowly. They hadn't been very deep to begin with, so it was just another few seconds before they both broke the surface together.

She blinked and choked, dragging heaving gulps of air into her lungs.

"Where did it go?" She clutched at his arms, peering into the water beneath them.

Despite the sunshine still beaming high in the sky, the sea seemed to have gotten dark and ominous looking. She expected to see the shark speeding up at them from below, jaws open wide, jagged teeth ready to clamp down on her leg. She shivered.

"Stay calm," he said, arms around her. Their legs bumped together as they treaded water. "The more erratic your movements, the more that guy is going to get curious and decide he needs to check you out again."

"It rubbed up against me!" She shivered. Out of the corner of her eye, she saw it again. A dark fin poking up from the surface between them and the boat. "Oh my God, Ben, there it is."

It was coming toward them…and then it was gone again, knifing into the water like a submerging submarine.

"Ben!"

He cupped her face in his hands until she looked back at him, then he readjusted her mask. "Can you handle going back down below? Will you be able to stay calm?"

Stay calm? She wasn't calm now, how was she supposed

to be calm when she couldn't breathe and there was a shark after her?

He wasn't letting go of her. Since she probably didn't have any choice but to give it a shot, she finally nodded.

"We'll stay close enough to the surface to breathe through our snorkels."

"Okay," she said, not believing for a minute that it was going to be okay.

He smiled. "Don't worry. It's very unlikely the shark is going to care about us one way or another. We are not the kind of food it wants, and it knows that. Everything will be fine." He looked like he actually believed what he was saying, and the clamp around her chest loosened just enough for her to breathe without wheezing.

"We're going to go down and start swimming toward the boat nice and easy, all right?" he said. "Below the surface we'll look less like something it might feel the need to investigate again, but if we're thrashing about up here, it's going to want to check us out."

She nodded again. She supposed that made sense.

Ben fit his snorkel back into his mouth, so Liz did the same. She felt as if she'd forgotten everything she'd learned about breathing with the snorkel, and had to focus on pushing oxygen out by way of her mouth and pulling it back in the same way.

Ben gave her a thumbs-up and squeezed her hand. He maintained eye contact and physical contact with her until they submerged, and then he let go and urged her forward.

Breathe. Breathe. Breathe.

The shark had disappeared once more, but this time she didn't look for it, because she knew she'd only start to panic if she saw it again. Instead, she kept the boat in her sights. Kicking her feet and pulling her arms forward and back, she started to close the distance.

Her muscles burned, and her head ached. Her limited swimming ability was being sorely tested after being in the water for so long. She couldn't decide if she would have gotten tired faster if they'd been on the surface doing the front crawl, or whether it was worse to swim this way—so much slower—knowing that the shark could rush them at any second.

About two hundred feet left.

The shark was back.

She jerked and reared back as it swam in front of her from the left. Ben put his hands on her waist and kept her from flailing. He squeezed, reminding her to hold it together.

It swam in front of them again before circling around. There was no doubt it was curious, but she had to admit, it didn't look rabid with hunger.

It had a wide strip of dark gray covering the top of it, but a white underbelly. To her it looked like Jaws, maybe not as big. Still, it was big enough that it was at least as long as she was tall, with cold black eyes that looked too huge for its head, a broad rounded snout, and those fins that scared her almost as much as the teeth she glimpsed in its partly opened mouth.

Ben took her hand again, pulling her with him now as he kept up a steady pace toward the boat. Shaking off bloody images of her dead body being ripped apart by jagged rows of knife-sharp teeth, she tugged her hand free and swam on her own. He stayed right beside her the whole time, and she kept her eyes on their destination.

Almost there.

Almost there.

She repeated it in her head, and then she *was* there, reaching for the ladder and pulling herself up and out of the water as fast as she could with flippers on her feet.

She tumbled over the edge of the boat and collapsed on the bench seat. She quickly shoved the mask and snorkel off her face before spinning back around to make sure Ben—

He was right there, mask already pushed up on top of his head, flippers on the top rung of the ladder. *Thank God.*

With a hand pressed to her chest, she gazed into the water as Ben sat down beside her. The shark had followed them right up to the hull of the boat.

As she watched, it turned away, making a wide circle around the area she and Ben had been swimming in. As if it didn't have a care in the world, it slowly zigzagged back and forth a little bit before heading out toward the shallows of the reef, where it disappeared once and for all.

"Wow." She glanced up at Ben. "That was…" She shook her head, speechless. Unsure how to explain what she was feeling. Now that she was safely in the boat and it was all sinking in…

Ben reached up and wiped the wet hair off her forehead, his fingers leaving tingles across her skin. He frowned. "I'm sorry. I shouldn't have brought you out here. I thought—"

"That was the most amazing thing I've ever done." Yes, it had also been one of the craziest, scariest moments of her life…but she wouldn't take it back now for anything.

"The sharks here are rarely aggressive, but I still should have warned you."

"Maybe," she admitted with a grin. "But if you had, I

probably wouldn't have come. And then I wouldn't have this unbelievable memory to take back home with me."

He suddenly smiled. "Then I'm glad I could help you build some new memories today."

Her head was still spinning, her blood still pumping. She didn't want the feeling to end. The vibe between them flipped just like that, her fingers twitching to reach out for the strong, gorgeous man in front of her.

Taking a deep breath, she got up on her knees and threw her leg over his lap. She knew he was the one who could keep those feelings alive and give her new, more intense sensations. She wanted that more than anything.

Battling a surge of shyness, she wet her lips. "I don't think I'm done building new memories," she whispered. "Not just yet."

She placed her palms on the rise of his hard pecs, her heart skipping when his muscles jumped beneath her touch. She curled her fingernails into his bare skin, still wet, but warm from the sun. Water droplets tracked down his torso to the waistband of his swim trunks, and she smiled.

His arms came around her. Water pooled on the cushion under her knees, but the breeze had picked up and dried their skin quickly—probably turning her curly hair into a damp, frizzy halo. But she wasn't cold, not even though she had shivers. Far from it.

"Beth." His voice was little more than a groan.

His gaze dropped to her mouth.

"Ben." Her voice was hoarse, the word burning all the way up her throat as much as his touch on her waist burned all the way to the core of her.

He watched her, his gaze suddenly smoking with

intensity. Slowly, he pushed his fingers into her hair and tugged her closer until her chest pressed against his.

He kissed her, tentatively and gentle. But her heart pounded too hard for gentle, the adrenaline raced too fast in her veins for gentle. She kissed him back with her whole body. Her arms wrapped around his neck, her thighs tightening over his hips. She gasped his name as his mouth traveled down the column of her throat, leaving a trail of heat more penetrating than the sun's bright rays.

When he pulled back she held her breath, waiting for what would come next. But he hesitated.

"Look at me," he said.

She snapped her eyes open, not even realizing she'd clenched them shut.

...

She tasted like strawberries and sunshine, and he was going crazy with wanting her.

He'd been on the edge of sanity all afternoon, and now she was throwing him over it. It didn't help that she'd climbed right onto his lap, her arms and thighs tight around him, hair falling around her shoulders in a halo, teasing the sides of his face as he kissed her. Her scent soaked into him, cocooning him in her sweetness and warmth, infusing his very soul with it.

He tightened the reins on his need and drew a finger down her cheek. "Are you sure? Maybe we should talk before this goes too far."

She bit her lip and her smile wobbled. He could shoot himself for killing the mood, but as much as he wanted her kisses and her body, he wanted something else even more. Something more than just an island fling.

He rejected the thought as quickly as it formed in his mind because... *Hell no*. He'd already gone down that road once before and been burned. And that was fine; he was over it. But not since he was a kid had anyone ever been given the opportunity to reject Ben Harrison more than once, for any reason.

She shook her head. "I'm not interested in talking," she said with a sigh of disappointment. "It's been such a wonderful day, and I'm still building island memories to take home with me."

His relief was sharp. He could give her that. A few memories to take back to her practical, ordered little life.

She was insistent, arching against him like a cat. He groaned and dragged his tongue down the smooth column of her sweetly bared neck before it was even a conscious decision. As his mouth moved to the delicate spot behind her ear, she shuddered, and he tightened his fists into the hollow of her spine.

Good God. He could shove down the front of his shorts and, with a strategic shift of the flimsy scrap of her red bikini bottoms to one side, be inside her right here, right now.

But that would be too easy, over too quickly.

No, she wanted to build a memory? He'd give her one she would carry with her for the rest of her days. One that would haunt her in the dark and set her pulse racing during the daylight hours.

He'd give them both a memory to hold onto when this moment in paradise was over and they had to return to the cold loneliness of reality.

What a cheerless thought for such a provocative moment. He shoved it aside and plundered her mouth with his tongue as he reached up her back and tugged apart the thin ties of her bikini top.

She stiffened for a fraction of a second, but then melted against him just as quickly. The front of her was plastered up against his chest, sticky with sea water and sweat, but he shifted her back an inch or two and deliberately peeled away the wet fabric. It plopped to the deck with a distinct splat, but neither of them much cared.

Ben looked into her twinkling eyes and took in her swollen wet lips before expanding his vision to the beauty of her stunning breasts. She had a hint of a tan line in a distinctly triangular pattern from a day spent frolicking in the sun, but her skin was still too pale, not that it took away from her perfection. She was a goddess made of flesh, too exquisite for words.

Cupping the weight of her breasts, he leaned down and took a tight, pebbled nipple against his tongue, rubbing it until her fingers dug into his hair, and she made delicious little sounds in the back of her throat.

He licked and sucked, molding her breasts to his palms. She undulated over his lap with the skill of a practiced exotic dancer until he could almost imagine he felt the heavy beat of club music pounding in his chest.

It wasn't his imagination. Some movement out of the corner of his eye drew his attention. Almost too late, he realized they were no longer alone. Another boat was closing in. Twice the size of theirs.

Beth jerked and tried to pull away, but he met her gaze and held her closer, pressing her chest flush against his. If she got up now, they'd only be putting on more of a show for their uninvited guests.

Even though the other boat had slowed before pulling up to their stern, the little bit of wake set him and Beth rocking against one another in time with the jostling boat, and he bit off a groan.

Her cheeks were red, and she tugged her bottom lip into her mouth, but there was also a twinkle of humor in her eyes. "Well, I did say I wanted memories, didn't I?" She giggled and ducked her head into the curve of his shoulder.

The music from the other boat blared. High-pitched electronic sounds mixed with a thunderous bass that cut through his passionate haze. He couldn't believe he hadn't heard the music long before these guys had crawled right up beside them.

"Hey dudes!" A male voice called down from their deck. Ben twisted his head to look over his shoulder at the young shirtless guy leaning over the railing and waving to them. "Why don't you come aboard and party with us?"

Beth lifted her head from his shoulder. "Oh my God," she whispered. "They're topless!"

She was referring to the three young blondes standing beside the guy, all of them dressed in white bikini bottoms and nothing else.

He raised a brow and chuckled. "So are you, my dear."

She smirked. "Is that supposed to make me feel better?"

"Safety in numbers?" He shouldn't be teasing her, but it felt good.

She glared at him and shook her head, but her green eyes sparkled.

He shrugged. "You sure you don't want to join them up there? I bet there'll be dancing, and I have to admit I could spend the rest of the afternoon watching you dance topless."

She instinctively pinned her body closer to his as if she could completely disappear from sight, but he wasn't about to object if it kept her on top of him.

A muffled sound from the dashboard of the boat caught his attention. *Cell phone.* Damn it, the calls were coming in more frequently. His gaze shifted the barest iota, but she must have noticed because she stiffened in his lap.

"We should probably start heading back," she murmured.

He wasn't ready for the afternoon to end. With a forced chuckle, he tightened his arms around her, looking back up at the people on the larger boat. "Thanks, guys." He called with a wave. "But we're good. Having our own private party down here, if you know what I mean."

Beth moaned and ducked her head again. He felt her chest shake with silent laughter.

Surfer dude gave him a big grin and a thumbs up. "Sure thing. See you two around!" All of them smiled and waved good-bye. One of the girls was so enthusiastic about it she… jiggled.

When the boat was far enough away that its passengers were unlikely to get an eyeful if they happened to still be watching, Beth awkwardly got up. Ben held on a fraction of a second too long, and felt the tug when she kept on going. His heart wanted to ask her to stay and continue what they'd started, but she ducked her head and turned away. It was obvious the moment between them was lost.

"I think we should head back." she said again. "I suppose we become business competitors again tomorrow, and there's a lot to prepare before the convention begins."

Well, shit. So much for the memories.

Chapter Seven

A few minutes later, Beth stood in the cramped space below deck with her bikini top in one hand and her arms crossed over her chest. Her cheeks were still burning, but oddly enough she couldn't wipe the crazy grin off her face.

Oh. My. God.

She held tight to herself as the adrenaline wore off. She thought of the look in Ben's eyes before he'd been distracted by his ringing cell phone, the look that had promised more than a reckless make-out session in the open air, something much hotter than even the sun beating down over them.

A bat of her eyes would have done it. Maybe a hitch in her breathing. Or a soft roll of her hips. He would have taken her. She'd been right there with him, to tell the truth. Boating and snorkeling had been a great adventure, but the only adventure that truly interested her involved…him. He was the ultimate adventure for her, and it scared the crap out of her.

Today had been fun, but it was just one day and, unfortunately, she knew who Ben *really* was. It was hard to forget when his work followed them even out into the middle of the ocean. He'd done a good job of ignoring it for a short time, but a man so focused on his career would never be able to let anything hold priority over it for long.

Leaning forward in front of the small mirror, she saw how red her nose was. Along with her cheeks, forehead, and shoulders. Not enough sunscreen. The sun and sea water had done more than put some color in her face, too. She squinted in the mirror, but the dim lighting did nothing to hide the fact that her hair was a frizzy, tangled mess worthy of Medusa.

And yet, it was the sparkle in her eyes that caught her attention.

With a start, she noticed her bikini top was dripping on the plush carpeting. She looked back and forth for somewhere to put it and finally just put it back on instead, breaking out into a shiver as the cold wet fabric covered her breasts.

She plopped down on the edge of the bed. *Hey, there's a bed down here.*

She wasn't going to think about the bed right now. Wasn't going to think about Ben's mouth, or his hands, or the hard length of him digging into her belly as she'd straddled him. She wasn't going to think about the way it had felt to peel herself off his lap, and know without a shadow of doubt that his eyes had been on her until she was all the way below deck. She wasn't going to even consider calling him down here and joining her on the bed for the rest of the afternoon.

She went back up on deck a few minutes later and calmly

suggested once more that they head back. The short boat ride to the harbor and the drive back to the resort passed with fewer than a dozen words spoken between them. After leaving the Jeep with the valet at the hotel, they made their way through the lobby to the elevators. When the doors slid open, they stepped inside and Ben punched the button for the third floor.

"What about you? What floor?" he asked.

"I'm on the same floor."

The door was sliding closed on an elevator empty except for the two of them. The small compartment seemed to get smaller the longer Ben's gaze remained fixed on her.

If the ride had been any more than three floors, she knew she would have ended up in his arms, backed up against the elevator wall. No doubt about it.

She remembered how good it had felt to have his body pressed against hers, his mouth devouring her. But now they were back on land, and she was starting to come back to her senses.

Even leaving aside their history, how could she possibly risk getting involved with someone who was openly competing for the same investment dollars as she was? Ultimately, they were both here to help their fledgling businesses succeed, and that's what she should be focusing on, because it was a sure bet that Ben Harrison wasn't going to let personal entanglements keep him from getting what *he* wanted. In fact, the entire day had no doubt been a tactic to distract *her*. She was glad that Daniel had seen through it, and she reminded herself to call him as soon as she got back to her room to see how he'd managed.

Thankfully, the doors of the elevator were opening again.

Liz took a deep breath and stepped out into the hallway.

"I'll walk you to your room," he said beside her, his voice a low rumble that sounded too good for her peace of mind.

She busied herself rummaging through her beach bag. Her room was second to the last at the end of the hall. When she stopped in front of the door, she had her key card in her hand and Ben was chuckling.

"What's so funny?" she asked.

"I suppose we could call it fate."

"What's fate?" She frowned.

He had a key card in his hand, too, and motioned to the corner room right next door to hers. "That's my room."

"It is?" Crap. She immediately started reviewing the business conversations she'd had in her room. Could he have heard anything through the walls?

He stepped closer, and she inched backward until her shoulders touched the door. He braced one hand on the doorjamb right above her head. Her gaze fixed on his mouth. She toyed with the idea of inviting him in. This man was her drug of choice, and she was so very close to falling off the wagon.

"Thanks for today," he said with a lazy smile. "I'll see you tomorrow, and we'll go over our ideas for the seminar and luncheon speech."

She stifled the sudden let-down feeling. She shouldn't be disappointed that he wasn't going to ask to see her tonight. She had to remember that the outing today wouldn't even have happened without Ms. Denham's intervention. This was a one-off, a fluke…a fantasy. Now it was over. Time to get back to real life. And her real life hadn't included Ben for a while now.

She forced her best business nod. "Of course. Give me a call in the morning, and we'll discuss it."

She waited for him to move back, but he didn't.

"Was there something else?" She pressed her shoulders against the hotel room door, looking no higher than the open collar of his shirt where his smooth bronzed skin showed through. She didn't want him to see how flustered she felt.

When he didn't say anything, she glanced up nervously to find him watching her. He reached out and drew the strap of her sundress gently up her shoulder. She hadn't even noticed it had slipped down. Goose bumps spread along her arm.

"What is it?" she asked.

His forehead creased. "I guess tomorrow we become competitors."

She laughed. "We majored in the same field in college and spent so much time together sharing ideas, I think we've always been competitors. But it never meant that we couldn't be friends before."

"Friends." The word came out sounding flat. "You certainly don't kiss like any of my other friends."

She bit her lip. "Ah, that was probably a mistake."

"Probably," he agreed, "but it's a mistake I wouldn't think twice about making again. In fact, I've been thinking about that mistake every moment since it happened."

"Ben, I—"

"And you've been thinking the same thing, too. Admit it."

Why not admit it? He hadn't called, or even sent an email, since she'd rejected his kiss, his partnership, and he left Seattle. He'd obviously decided that if he couldn't have what he wanted from her, he didn't need anything, which meant their friendship was never as strong as she'd believed. Why not let it go completely and accept the fact that the only thing they'd ever have between them again was this possibility of a cheap island fling?

Part of her was immensely disappointed by that, but another part, the part that had spent a sizzling afternoon being tortured by his near nakedness and seduced by his blistering kisses, would take Ben Harrison's body in a heartbeat, and so she shoved the rest aside.

"Why don't you take me to dinner tonight, and find out exactly what I've been thinking?" She was impressed with her daring, even as she felt the hot blush spread across her cheeks.

He groaned. "You have no idea how much I want to do just that, but I can't tonight. I promised Steve I'd meet up with him. We have a lot to get caught up on if I'm going to spend the next few days working on these presentations with you."

"Oh, of course." She swallowed, all the sauciness and bravery she'd just reveled in melting away. "I'll see you tomorrow, then."

"Definitely."

• • •

Liz closed the door behind her and leaned up against it, taking deep breaths, but she didn't have much time to think, because there was a knock at the door.

She sighed and turned back around to answer it, not really surprised to see her brother standing there. "Hi there, were you waiting for me to get back?"

"I tried calling a couple of times. I kind of expected you back earlier." Daniel pushed past her into the room. He sounded flustered.

She put a hand on her hip. "Are you checking up on me?"

"I just wanted to make sure you would be back in time for the meeting."

She frowned. "What meeting?"

"The one I made with Diego Vargas for this evening."

"He's here? You talked to him already?"

He chuckled. "I told you I'd get the job done while you were gone. I ran into him as he was checking into the hotel and introduced myself." There was a sparkle in Daniel's eyes. "He made it clear that he's interested in what we've been working on, Liz. Very interested."

"That sounds wonderful," she said with a surge of nervous excitement. She started running her presentation through her head. "And he wants to meet with us tonight?"

"In the restaurant at eight. Actually, it's just going to be the two of you…well, if you don't mind. I kind of had something else I was going to do."

"You have plans?"

He gave her a cheeky grin. "I met someone today out at the pool, just like you did yesterday."

"Oh, okay then." She punched him in the upper arm. "Um, don't do anything I wouldn't do?"

Daniel grimaced. "I don't really want to think about what you would or wouldn't do."

She laughed. "Right, and that goes both ways. So get out of my room now, and I'll talk to you tomorrow."

"Good luck with Vargas." In the doorway, he paused. "Are you sure it's okay—"

She put her hand on the same arm, but not to punch him this time. "Don't worry, it'll be fine. I can handle this one on my own."

A few hours later, she walked into the dining room of the hotel, ready to do just that.

The hostess led her through the restaurant. When she stopped in front of a booth off in a quiet corner, a man stood to greet her. He straightened his dark, tailored suit and a perfectly knotted tie, and she was glad she'd worn her little black dress, even though it was nothing flashy.

He held out his hand with a smile that smoothed out the lines in his face, making him look much younger than she'd expected of someone running a company as successful and diversified as Jemarcho.

"Ms. Carlson?"

"Mr. Vargas, thank you for meeting with me tonight." She shook his hand and then took the seat across from him.

"Your brother was most convincing when he approached me this afternoon. How could I refuse?" He smiled. "And I don't even let my secretary call me Mr. Vargas. It's just Diego. Please."

"Well then, I'm definitely just Liz."

"Nice to meet you," he said. "I've ordered some wine. I hope that's all right with you."

"Of course." She took a deep breath, gearing up to wow the pants off "just Diego" with her pitch. "So, let me tell you a little bit about Sharkston Co. and the programming we've been working on."

She was waylaid as the waitress stopped at their table

with a bottle of wine and two glasses. She poured a sample into one of the glasses and handed it to Diego, but he shook his head. "Allow the lady to decide."

She took a sip. "Oh, that's wonderful."

When the waitress had poured more wine for each of them and left them alone again, she said, "You have fantastic taste in wine."

He laughed. "I was surprised to find it on the list so far away from home, but I always support the family business whenever I can." He raised his glass to toast. "This is from my sister's winery."

She tipped her own glass. "Please let her know that she's won a new customer."

"She'll be glad to hear it." They clinked glasses and took another sip of wine. "So, I understand that your company is a family venture as well," he said.

She nodded, glad for the opening. "My brother and I started it together, and together we've developed a machine learning program that will revolutionize targeted internet marketing."

"There are already programs that can read browser histories and target advertising accordingly."

She leaned forward eagerly. "Yes, but all of them are site-specific, which limits what they can read and how they can react. I can promise that my program's AI is more advanced than anything currently available."

He nodded. "I've been investigating the capabilities of this type of technology for quite a while, and for the most part, I have to say that you're probably right about the limitations of its current adaptations." He tapped his finger on the tabletop. "But I've recently heard some good things about another company, one which is claiming to be able to offer similar programming as yours."

"Optimus Inc." Her stomach tightened, but she forged ahead, determined to convince Diego to bet on her instead of Ben Harrison. "Mr. Harrison's company has some great ideas, but he hasn't got what you're looking for."

"Why do you say that?"

She took a deep breath and went for it. "Because I've done my research, Mr. Vargas—er, Diego. Your company is reaching wider and wider for new customers. Sharkston Co. can be the massive net that goes everywhere and sees everything. We can capture them all for you."

He looked at her carefully. "You seem pretty confident about that."

"I am," she said firmly. "I promise that nobody will be able to meet your company's needs like Sharkston."

Diego looked her up and down, as if weighing her words against the conviction in her voice...and probably in her face.

A heady thrill rushed through her. This was her first big pitch, her first real negotiation for Sharkston Co., and it felt great. She knew she was right, knew her program was just what Diego Vargas needed.

"I'm interested," he said with a nod. "Why don't we talk again before the convention ends?"

She grinned. "Of course."

"Get me your portfolio and a demo to look over in the meantime?"

"First thing in the morning, maybe sooner." She grinned and smacked her palm on the table with excitement.

Diego laughed, making her blush. She looked up to see

if anyone else had witnessed her lapse in cool and her smile froze. At a small, intimate corner table across the room sat Ben Harrison with a devastatingly gorgeous blonde who was definitely not his business partner. There was a candle between them, much like the candle on her table, but as the light revealed how happy he seemed to be, how much he was enjoying himself, her stomach twisted.

It was Meredith Stone.

She tried to look away and smiled back at Diego again. She felt the strain pulling at her cheeks, but hoped it didn't show. "So how do you like Antigua?" she asked brightly.

"I thought it would be all sunshine and snorkeling here in the islands, but I hear we might have something of a storm on its way in."

Her gaze slipped away again. Ben was dressed more formally tonight than he'd been with her last night, in a suit with a tie. And his...*date* wore a sleek red gown that showed off every curve she had and put Liz's simple black dress to shame.

"—before it comes."

She jerked back to Diego with a start. "I'm so sorry, what did you say?"

He looked from her out into the dining room curiously, but refrained from saying anything about the distraction she obviously hadn't been able to hide. "Is there somewhere else you need to be this evening?" he asked.

"What? No, of course not. I thought I saw...someone... at one of the other tables, but it's...nobody."

His smile was friendly and open. "Well then, say you'll join me for dinner tonight? I was busy fielding emergency calls from the office earlier and haven't had a chance to eat yet."

"I'd love to." She refused to look at Ben again and picked up her wineglass. "Why don't I tell you about our distribution projections? We're hoping that—"

His expression was warm as he stopped her. "Quitting time was hours ago even back in the city, so I vote that we call a hiatus on the business talk for the rest of the night. What do you think, Ms. Carlson?"

"Liz," she reminded him with a laugh. "And I think you're absolutely right."

"So why don't you tell me what you like to do for fun?" He leaned forward, focusing only on her.

Chapter Eight

Ben winced. Was that Beth's warm, husky voice tumbling his way, or was he deluding himself that he could hear it from across the busy restaurant? He looked over. She and Diego Vargas were leaning close to one another over an intimate table for two. Beth was smiling and talking animatedly about something. She looked gorgeous in a slim black dress with her hair down. Sexy and vibrant and…like she was having the best date of her life.

"Ben?"

He blinked and turned back to Meredith. "I wish I'd known you were coming," he said. "Why didn't Nolan say anything?"

She laughed. "And miss the look on your face when I showed up outside your hotel room?" She cocked her head. "You know, now that I think about it, that wasn't just happy surprise to get a visit from a friend. I think I saw a little bit of disappointment there. Could it be that you were hoping I was someone else?"

He heard Beth's throaty chuckle again and clenched his jaw as he imagined her smiling into the other man's eyes.

"Of course I was expecting someone else." He grinned when Meredith crossed her arms and sputtered. "The room service guy was just about to bring me a really great sandwich."

She reached over the table and punched him in the arm. "If you didn't want to come to dinner, you should have said something."

"I *did* say something. I said I was working."

"Well, I'm hungry, and I didn't want to wait in my room alone for Steve to be ready."

"Don't get me wrong, I appreciate the company, but why did he ask you to come to Antigua?"

"He didn't tell you?"

"Tell me what?"

She scrunched up her nose. "He got himself in a sticky situation with a reporter. I guess he wanted me here to run interference so he wouldn't have to watch his back while the two of you are trying to do business."

"Situation?"

"The reporter is a leggy blonde." She raised a sculpted eyebrow. "Do you really have to ask?"

He groaned. "What happened this time?"

She shrugged a delicate shoulder. "The usual. He played the devastating bad boy, the girl fell hopelessly in love. Now he can't bring himself to break her heart, so he's been avoiding her instead. Trouble is, this one hasn't gotten the hint, and since she's a reporter, she just happens to show up wherever he is in the guise of researching a story."

"So she actually came here to the convention? Is she even with any of the industry publications?"

"I have no idea who she is or where she's from. In fact, I only agreed to this because I didn't want to be home this week anyway."

"Your father—"

"You mean the Dictator?"

Ben shook his head. "Have you even been in the same room with the guy since—"

"No, and it's not going to happen any time soon if I have something to say about it, either."

"You do realize you're just as stubborn as he is."

She glared at him. "If you compare that man to me one more time, I will never speak to you again."

"Promise?" He laughed.

"Don't joke." She pouted. "You and Steve are all I have now."

He took her hand and squeezed. "You know I'll always be your friend, Mer. But one of these days you'll have to work this out with him."

She waved him off. "Well, when that day comes I'll let you know. But right now I'm perfectly happy playing the fake girlfriend for Steve and watching you schmooze all these corporate bigwigs." She sat back and looked around the room with an assessing eye. "So which one of them are you going after first?"

He instinctively glanced back at Beth again as he saw her get up from the table from the corner of his eye. This time Meredith noticed where he was looking. "Which one has the investment dollars?" she asked. "The deliciously hot Spanish dude, or the gorgeous redhead?"

"Her name is Beth," he said, frowning as Vargas rose with her and helped wrap her scarf around her shoulders. She laughed over her shoulder at something he said, and he put his hand on her lower back as they started to walk out of the restaurant.

Beth didn't look in Ben's direction once.

He jerked his gaze away with a muttered oath.

"I see."

"Oh? What do you see?"

"This is the same Beth that turned you down before you left Seattle, isn't it?"

He swore. He didn't even remember telling her that, so she must have heard it from Nolan. "She didn't turn me down."

"Then what are you calling it?"

"We were friends. That's all."

"Right. I'm your friend, too, remember, but you didn't ask me to move to New York with you."

"You already live in New York."

"Don't be a smart ass. And don't evade. It doesn't look good on you."

He sighed. "This is none of your business, and I'm done talking about it."

"Fine," she said in a too-cheerful voice. "Then tell me who the guy is with her."

"Diego Vargas, president of Jemarcho."

"Is she buttering him up for money the same as you?"

"We're soliciting interest from savvy industry professionals for investment opportunities," he clarified. "I don't know what she's doing," he admitted, feeling surly. If this had been a business meeting, wouldn't she have brought her partner along?

A hand tapped him on the shoulder. "Hey, was that Elizabeth Carlson I just saw leaving with Vargas?" Nolan walked around the table and pulled up a chair beside Meredith. "We're scheduled to meet with him tomorrow. Do you think we need to be worried that she got to him first?"

Ben stood from the table and buttoned his jacket. "I'm not worried. We knew we weren't going to be the only company courting him. Jemarcho Inc. is looking for something only we can give; it just doesn't know it yet." He forced a smile. "Having said that, I have some work to do, so why don't you two have dinner without me? I think I'll go back upstairs to my room service sandwich."

After leaving the restaurant, though, instead of heading to the elevators he took the first door leading outside and found himself next to the open-air bar. There were more people milling around out here than there had been inside, but he wasn't in the mood to mingle and went in the opposite direction, following a little garden path dimly lit with lanterns.

"Ben?"

Beth.

He turned to see her sitting on a white bench under the shadowy canopy of a large cinnamon tree. The bench had been tucked away just out of sight of the main path, shrouding her in darkness, but for a sliver of moonlight that ghosted across her cheek.

She was alone.

She looked pensive and too beautiful for words.

He stuffed his hands in his pants pockets and leaned against the tree. "What happened to your date?"

She cocked her head to the side and looked up at him.

"What about *yours*?"

So she *had* noticed him back in the restaurant. "Not a date," he said. "Are you negotiating with Diego Vargas for investment contributions for your company?"

She frowned. "Are we going to have a problem if I am?"

"I can handle it if you can," he said with a toothy smile.

She grinned back at him, but he thought she looked a little nervous. "I thought you could."

She got up and swung her little purse over her shoulder. "Well, I guess I had better—"

"Walk with me," he said, letting the mood take him. He read her moment of hesitation and added, "Unless you're tired. I know it's been a long day."

"I'm fine. I just…what is it we're doing here?" She shook her head.

He thought of the way he'd felt watching her with Vargas in the restaurant, feelings that had nothing to do with business, or friendship. Feelings he'd been trying to reject just like she'd rejected him a year ago.

"Whatever it is has been coming for a long time now, Beth." He reached for her hand.

The look in her eyes was wide and vulnerable, spearing him in the gut. He realized that he could hurt her if he wasn't careful, but he also knew that wouldn't stop him from taking this chance. "Don't you think it's time we stopped fighting it and see where it can take us?"

Chapter Nine

She looked at his outstretched hand, seeing it for what it was. A challenge. An invitation. A promise.

Liz had certainly been deluding herself when she thought she could handle having a fling with Ben Harrison. It couldn't happen. They could never be just a "fling." A fling was something you didn't put your heart into.

She took his hand.

He was right. Back in Seattle, she had valued her friendship with him so much that she'd never allowed herself to acknowledge when what she'd felt had turned into something more than just friendship. She'd denied her own wants and desires to protect that friendship. To protect herself from being hurt by him the way she'd been hurt before.

And everything had changed anyway.

So now she was going to do exactly what she'd contemplated since seeing him poolside yesterday afternoon—let go of the past and just focus on the here and now.

They made their way through the secluded little pathway leading to a short rock wall near the edge of the beach.

She thought about how quickly winter was coming back home. The leaves had turned color and already lay moldering in the damp streets. The tree branches looked like emaciated wraiths creaking in the wind. Seattle wouldn't actually get much snow, if any. There'd been a blizzard once last year that dumped the white stuff down overnight, caused havoc on the roads in the morning, and had been gone by lunch time. No, come wintertime, snow wasn't the problem. It was the dreary, constant rains that made everything cold and gray and damp. Depressing.

Here the sun shone like a beacon of contentment during the day, and the moon looked like a glowing opal in the night sky. She couldn't imagine the weather ever being anything other than perfect.

Liz breathed deeply. The air felt like freedom, and she drew it in, letting it coat her insides. She was a little upset that she'd missed the sunset. The stars glittered, tiny specks of diamond against black velvet. Hard to believe it was the same sky that was so often obscured by clouds back in her neck of the woods.

She hadn't been out to the beach since arriving on the island, and the crashing surf called to her. She couldn't resist and didn't want to. Her heart beat faster as she glanced at Ben.

With a small smile, she walked through the open gate in the wall. Her tall, narrow heels slipped into the sand like hot spikes through butter, sending her off balance. Carefully, she bent and took them off. Holding them by the straps in one hand along with her clutch, she walked out a little further, digging her toes in the sand. It was still warm from a day under the hot sun.

"Isn't this wonderful?" She sighed with pleasure and looked over her shoulder with a smile.

He waited just behind her, leaning one hip against the wall. His gaze never left her. "You're pretty wonderful," he finally said.

She felt the flush that went all the way down her body, but the memory of him sitting across a table from the beautiful Meredith Stone was still close. He'd said it wasn't a date, but she knew she didn't have all the information about the two of them.

She looked him up and down with a sigh.

"What is it?" he asked.

"I wish we could take a walk along the beach, but it's getting late. Tomorrow will be busy; we'll have a lot of work to do." He looked ridiculously amazing, but that suit wouldn't last long against the sand and surf.

When he bent down to remove his socks and shoes and rolled his pant legs up to mid-shin, she laughed. He straightened, holding his shoes with two fingers.

Feeling suddenly carefree, she let her sandals swing from her fingers and started walking, delighting in the sand between her toes and the breeze that tossed her hair across her face. When Ben fell into step beside her and took her hand, she thought she'd never been happier than in this moment.

They came across a flagstone path leading to a little greenhouse surrounded by a small hedge. Liz rushed forward and peered through the glass, squinting to see beyond the shadows to the greenery inside. "It's so strange to find a greenhouse right here on the beach," she said. "But isn't it gorgeous?"

Ben pulled open the door and motioned for her to go inside. "Oh no, we shouldn't," she said, holding her breath.

"Why not?"

"I don't think this is part of the resort. What if we get caught trespassing on someone else's property?"

He looked around at the deserted beach. "I promise to break you out of prison if it becomes necessary," he teased. "But I doubt anyone will mind if we just take a quick look inside."

That was so…Ben. Reckless and bold, daring her to keep up with him.

Liz paused inside the screen door, still nervous about the idea of intruding on someone else's private space, but the rush of steamy air and sweet perfumes pulled her another step forward. And another. Ben found a lantern and some long wooden matches on a worktable. When he lit it, the greenhouse came alive with soft colors.

Soon she was lost in the beautiful plumeria and allamanda. She ran her finger very gently over the tight bud of a deep red rose and marvelled at the different colors of bougainvillea falling out of pots hanging from the low ceiling.

She spun around slowly and stopped in front of Ben with a sigh of wonderment. "Isn't this the most romantic place you've ever seen?" she whispered, afraid to destroy the magic she felt here with too much noise.

He came closer, twirling a hibiscus flower between his fingers. He dragged the petals across her cheekbone and tucked the stem behind her ear. In the low light, his eyes looked stormy and dark, as if they could barely hold back his intensity.

"I remember how much you love flowers."

"I still do," she admitted. "But it's so hard to keep anything green at home because I inevitably kill all my plants with neglect."

"Maybe you work too much," he murmured.

She raised an eyebrow. "This, coming from the man who *defines* the word 'workaholic'?"

"You're right. I don't even have time for fake plants." He chuckled like that wasn't the exact reason why the two of them could never be more than just a passing fancy.

As hard as she'd worked to start her business, she knew that she could put the time into it now because she didn't have a family to care for. But she *wanted* that family someday, and she absolutely refused to plan her life around a man whose career consumed his whole existence. It was one thing to neglect some houseplants, and quite another to break two innocent children's hearts with the same kind of neglect.

At the same time, she couldn't blame him for how he felt. He'd only ever mentioned his father to her once, during a rare moment of vulnerability back in college. He'd missed an entire day of classes, so she'd known something was up. Sure enough he'd been at home, sicker than a dog. His mom had been out of town and when Liz asked if there was anyone else who could stay with him, he'd recounted fragments of the tragic story as if he was halfway living it through a feverish dream. The rest she pieced together on her own.

Ben's mother had apparently written to the man with whom she'd had a wild but brief affair when she realized she was pregnant but never received any response, so she struggled to make ends meet on her own for her and her baby. Although they were never more than barely comfortable, the two of them managed. The boy turned out to be a gifted student, especially in computer science and economics, and during the summer after high school, with a full scholarship in his pocket and a bright future ahead of him, he'd optimistically decided to look his father up on his own.

Liz had pictured the hopeful posture of a proud young man approaching the father he'd been dreaming about his entire life. But the asshole hadn't even given him a chance. He'd rejected Ben's very existence and threatened to sue for defamation if either he or his mother ever contacted him again.

"What's the matter?" he asked.

She blinked and plastered the smile back on her face. He touched the flower at her ear and let his fingers trail slowly back down her cheek until the smile felt real again and she shivered with the need for him to touch her everywhere. "It's almost as beautiful as you are," he said.

She ducked her head and cleared her throat. "I suppose we should get out of here before someone sees the light and comes to investigate."

With a teasing grin at her paranoia, he followed her out of the greenhouse, and they continued on down the beach. They walked for a while, both of them quiet. Liz opened her mouth more than once to say something, anything, but each time she changed her mind, loathe to rupture the odd, relaxed mood that felt heartbreakingly nostalgic.

At the shoreline they stopped. The tide gently washed in and out, covering her coral-painted toes one minute and leaving them chilly and wet the next. Sand shifted under her feet like the world was falling away. She was going to need to wear this dress at least one more time and couldn't afford to buy a new one just because of a whimsical walk along the beach, so she backed away before the salt water could rise any higher than her toes.

She backed right into Ben and stumbled, but he caught her by the waist, his big hands riding up her rib cage.

"Back up," she screeched, lifting the hem of her skirt to her knees. "The water will ruin my dress."

He just laughed, and instead of helping her out of the water, he swung her up into his arms and waded in deeper. "What are you doing?" She threw her arm around his neck in a death grip. "You're going to ruin your suit, too."

"It's okay. I've got another one."

She smacked his arm with the flat side of her purse. "I'm sure it was expensive. Don't be an idiot. Put me down."

"Right now?" His eyes gleamed with mischief. They were shin deep in the sea. He started to drop her, his arms lowering. "All right. If you insist."

"No, wait! Over there." She pointed to a sandy rise away from the water line. "Please."

Ben shrugged and stepped back, arms tightening under her knees and behind her back until she was pressed so close to him she could hear his heart beating. When he stopped and let go of her legs, she found herself sliding all the way down the length of his powerful body.

Good lord. She shut her eyes and held her breath until she felt the wet sand beneath her feet.

"Is that better?" he asked in a husky voice, still holding her close.

She blinked and nodded. The lightly teasing atmosphere

between them had flipped so quickly into something else, something taught and heated. She was left breathless, unsure whether her legs would hold her, staring up at his mouth and wanting to be kissed so badly it was an ache.

"What's the real reason why you wouldn't come to New York with me?" he asked.

She had to think, search her brain for the meaning of each of his words and then piece them together, because as much as she'd been staring at his lips, she hadn't paid any attention to what was coming out of them.

With a shaky breath, she pushed away, took a half step back, and forced a grin. "Do we really have to talk about that?"

He ran his fingers softly down her arm, which was too red from the sun today. Had it only been a few hours ago that they'd been frolicking in the water in nothing more than their bathing suits?

From anyone else, the touch might have been innocent, but not from Ben. She recognized well enough that there was a wealth of meaning and intention in everything he did, the only question was whether or not she was willing to see it, accept it, respond to it.

"I know it wasn't because you didn't like the way I kissed you." He leaned down to kiss her again now, taking his time and proving to them both that she liked it very much. So much that she was gripping his arms and making little sounds of need in the back of her throat before he was done.

"That wasn't fair." She groaned at his tactics. "Maybe I didn't go to New York because I know you play dirty."

His gaze turned solemn, as if he could sense that she was only half joking. After what he'd gone through with Jeffrey

Olsen, she could see why that would be a sensitive issue for him.

"You want the truth?"

On either side of her face, his thumbs gently traced the line of her jaw as he looked down at her. "Always."

"You scared the crap out of me," she admitted. "You're on this speeding train heading right to the top of the world, and nothing's going to stand in your way until you get there. I knew it even then."

"You're not in my way, Beth. We're on that same train, aren't we? And there are enough seats in the captain's car for the both of us," he said with a crooked smile, obviously amused by her imagery.

She shook her head. "No, we aren't, Ben. We don't want the same things, and I knew it even then. I didn't want to hold you back."

He frowned and dropped his hands. "That's bullshit. I don't understand what you're—"

"I don't want to talk anymore." She crossed her arms. "I just want to make more of those memories we started earlier." His expression was tight. She knew how stubborn he could be when he was after answers, but the last thing she wanted was to spend this beautiful night rehashing the past between them. "Please," she begged. "Tonight has been so perfect. Let's not ruin it."

Finally, he stepped back and made an exaggerated bow in front of her. "Would you care to dance?"

Her heart skipped, and she looked around at the empty beach. "Here? There isn't any music."

He tapped her gently in the middle of the chest. "The music is there. You just have to listen for it."

A cloud had drifted in front of the bright moon, obscuring Ben's features as she stepped closer. She couldn't remember the last time she'd danced. He took her hand, and she automatically went up on her tiptoes, imagining the music. What came to mind wasn't soft or romantic, but aggressive, powerful, and fierce. A symphony of sound that drowned out her misgivings.

Heat flooded her system as his arm closed around her waist, and she didn't feel the cold water rushing over her toes anymore. All she felt were sparks. Sparks and lights. Enough to turn the whole island into the fourth of July.

It was a perfect symphony.

...

The breeze had picked up, drawing pieces of her hair behind her and leaving her nape and shoulders bare as he twirled her just to watch her laugh. The waves crashing on the beach matched the pounding of his heart, thundering with anticipation. When she spun to a stop, breathing hard, he pulled her close again and moved them to a slower beat so he could feel her slide against him.

He took her chin between his thumb and forefinger. Her breathing hitched and her eyelashes fluttered closed as he bent to cover her supple, glossy pink lips with his. The rush of molten heat and the sizzle of powerful electricity raised the hair on his arms. Her mouth parted as she tilted her face up and traced the shape of his lips with her tongue, surprising him with her boldness.

A year ago, he thought he'd had Beth Carlson all figured out. He hadn't even considered that she would say no to him when he kissed her. They'd been dancing around their attraction for one another for so long, it became laughably obvious to one and all. He'd actually thought he was doing them both a favor by kissing her and putting their feelings out there in the open. But he'd been wrong, and he was realizing that he'd been wrong about a lot of things.

Including that the reason she'd refused to go with him to New York had nothing to do with her deciding that he'd somehow betrayed their friendship by kissing her, and it had nothing to do with not wanting to get in the way of his career.

She'd been *afraid* then, and she was *still* afraid. He could see it in the spots of color blooming over her cheekbones and in the wary set of her jaw. He could feel it in the tension of her shoulders even as she danced with him.

He spread his hands over her spine and traced every one of her devastating curves through the thin material of her dress. His hands slowly dragged up to her shoulders, the back of her neck. He plunged his fingers into her silky hair, destroying what was left of her casual up-do.

Ben thought maybe he knew why Beth was afraid, but it didn't matter. A part of him might be disappointed she hadn't considered their friendship strong enough to trust him, but he quashed it. All that was history, and he didn't want to look back, only forward.

His grip on her upper arms tightened with the lies he told himself, but they were lies that had to become truth if he was going to stay in control. Beth could keep her personal demons if that's what she wanted, because he had his own to bear. The only thing that mattered was this. Here, right now. The night air. The crashing waves. The feel of her thighs against his. Her softness and his strength. The smell of sunshine in her hair. The taste of berries from her lips.

She clutched at his waist as he deepened the kiss and gave her his tongue, daring her to suck it, to rub her tongue along his until they were both panting.

She made a small sound, a moan that arrowed straight to his gut, giving him second thoughts about starting something out here on the beach.

Maybe she sensed his hesitation. She put her hands between them and leaned back, taking deep breaths. Her mouth glistened; her eyes sparkled. *So damn beautiful.* Beth embodied every dream he'd ever had, come to life in his arms. But dreams had a way of screwing with a person, so he banished them now, just like he had the moment he'd left Seattle, alone.

They made their way back to the resort, but not before stopping in the garden path just out of reach of the lanterns marking the edge of civilization. There, he kissed her senseless again just for good measure before walking her to the elevator.

They weren't lucky enough to get an empty elevator to the third floor, but he still couldn't keep his hands off her. The short ride took forever. As they stood side by side behind another couple, he held her hand, but it wasn't enough. His thumb made circles in the center of her palm. He reached up and wrapped one of her curls around his finger.

When they got off the elevator, she walked ahead. He felt like he was stalking her down the hall, eyes glued to the sway of her hips. The black dress slithered over her, and when she glanced over her shoulder with smiling invitation in her eyes, he couldn't wait to get it off her.

There was a man waiting in front of her door. *Fuck.*

"Daniel," said Beth. "What are you doing here? Is something wrong?"

The brother looked Ben up and down with a dark, suspicious scowl. It wasn't hard to imagine exactly what he was thinking. That Ben was a shark out to screw his sister — in one way or another. He didn't necessarily agree with the silent assassination of his character and of his intentions, but he could see where Daniel might not be entirely wrong to feel the way he did.

As they stopped in front of the door, Daniel subtly shifted so his back was to Ben, separating him from Beth. Ben saw through the move and put his shoulder to the wall with a small smile. He had no problem giving them some room, but he wasn't ready to leave yet, and from the nasty sideways glare Daniel sent his way, Ben had made that abundantly clear.

Beth quickly glanced up, too. He was glad for the sparkle in her eyes, because it meant that she, at least, knew he wasn't trying to screw with her.

"I wanted to talk to you about the meeting," said Daniel. "I didn't realize you had made another, uh…*date* with the competition."

He took Beth's arm and edged her farther away from Ben, leaning in to whisper, "Maybe we could talk *alone.*"

When Beth gave him an apologetic look, Ben only winked and crossed his arms, stubbornly settling in.

"Yeah, of course." She turned back to her brother, but a grin twitched at her lips. "Just give me a minute. Why don't you wait inside, and I'll be right there?"

She opened up the door to her room. Daniel paused,

tossing another glare Ben's way, but he finally left them alone out in the hall.

"Do you think he's glued to the peep hole?"

Beth giggled and pulled him down the hall until they were in front of his own door. "Cut him a break. He's just watching out for me."

"And your company."

"And our company," she agreed with a teasing smile. "After all, we have to be careful about cavorting with the enemy."

He stepped closer. "Is that what we are?"

"What? Enemies?" Her gaze fixed on his mouth, and he watched as she pulled her bottom lip between her teeth. He'd been waiting for that all night.

He pulled her against him. "No...*cavorting*."

Chapter Ten

The next morning, Liz was pulled from a deep sleep by the shrill ring of the telephone.

She didn't excel at abrupt awakenings, and coordination wasn't her strongest trait at the best of times. The handset went tumbling out of her grasp and across the top of the nightstand as she sluggishly reached for it.

"Wait, don't hang up," she called. When she finally had the phone securely in her hand she flopped back into her pillow. "Daniel, why are you torturing me so early? I told you last night that—"

"Not Daniel." Ben's deep chuckle on the other end of the line perked her up, and she pushed herself to a sitting position and dragged a hand through her hair.

"Oh, sorry. I thought it was my brother thinking he could manipulate me while I was still half asleep."

"Does he often try to manipulate you?"

"He means well, but he's a…worrier." She groaned.

"Why are you calling me so damn early, anyway?"

"Still not a morning person, I see." He sounded way too cheerful. She might have to kill him.

"How do you know if I'm a morning person or not?"

"I was the one who brought you coffee every day to get you out the door to morning classes, remember? If not for me, you'd never have gotten up in time."

"Says you," she grouched. She remembered those days, and although he might be right about her not being a morning person in general, he was wrong about one thing: she'd always been awake and anxiously waiting for his knock at her door. "But it just so happens that I was planning to take it easy this morning and—"

"What if I tell you I have coffee?"

"I'm listening." She pushed her hair out of her face and pulled her knees up to her chest beneath the blankets, trying not to think about how much better it would have been if he was here with her this morning, waking her up with kisses and the solid warmth of his body against hers. Unfortunately, Daniel had stayed longer than she expected, and when he left, she realized she wasn't bold enough to go next door and resume what they'd started. The second thoughts had already started to kick in.

"Laura from the convention committee has set aside one of the resort's small conference rooms for us. We'll make our product pitches in there this morning, but we'll also have access to it for the rest of the day to prepare for our seminar tomorrow. She'll provide whatever resources we need as well. After the pitches, why don't we meet in there for a while and get started?"

"Sure," she said. "That will give me a chance to go over

my seminar ideas with you."

"Perfect, I've got a few ideas, too."

"Great. See you later then."

She hung up, only to pick up the phone again to call Daniel. When he didn't answer she figured he was still asleep and left a message to let him know what the agenda was for the morning.

Today she had to get back to reality, and the reality was that she and Ben were competitors, and this was their arena. She couldn't forget it, and she couldn't let what might be happening between the two of them get in the way of it. Today her focus was the product pitches. Sharkston and Optimus Inc. were each holding open sessions to introduce themselves and their products to the convention attendees, so that tomorrow when she and Ben gave their workshop, everyone would already have a good idea where they were coming from, business-wise.

The pitches were also an important part of the competition, because the same attendees would be voting for either Sharkston or Optimus Inc. based on what they thought of the pitches, what they got out of the workshop, and the overall impression she and Ben made on their industry colleagues this week.

Ben and Steve Nolan would step up to make their pitch directly after her, which gave them an advantage. That meant Sharkston had to completely *rock* their time slot so that it wouldn't matter what Ben said afterward.

An hour later, she made her way downstairs to the registration desk with a fresh cup of coffee in hand. She looked for Daniel. He hadn't answered his phone, so she assumed he'd already gotten up and out to register for the convention.

The room was crowded and noisy, and four lines jutted out in front of the two long folding tables that were butted up against each other. As people started coming away with their information packets, hanging badges around their necks, she was able to recognize company names, if not everyone's individual names.

She greeted as many people as she could. What better way for them to remember her when it came time to vote than to stay front and center with a bright smile on her face?

With each introduction, she asked all of the attendees where they were from and what business they were in—unless she knew the answers already, in which case she made sure to ask something more pointed and insightful—then filed the information away in one of the many folders in her methodical mind where it would be easily accessed later. Only when she was asked in return, though, did she offer a brief description of her new company and what Sharkston planned to bring the industry.

She stuck out her hand and introduced herself to a VP from Magnatech named Elise whose head office was in her neck of the woods.

"You're one of the featured attendees," the woman said.

"Yes. My company specializes in advanced machine learning, AI programming, and analytics." Liz gave her best confident smile. She was doing a great job working the room so far, if she did say so herself. "And, if you'll forgive my boldness, I think we would be a perfect match for Magnatech's security engineering and information assurance applications."

"It definitely sounds like something Magnatech would be interested in negotiating." She smiled.

"My partner and I are pitching today in the small conference room. I'd love it if you came by to check it out."

"I'll do that, thanks," she said.

The hall rang out with the sound of laughter. It was coming from a large group near the entrance. She glanced over and realized that Ben was right in the middle of it, surrounded by men and women patting him on the back and shaking his hand. Her confidence wavered.

"Charismatic, isn't he?" Elise said, nodding in their direction. Ben was already in conversation with someone new. He had a hand stuffed in his pants pocket under his suit jacket, looking like a harmless playboy, but she knew it was all an act. He was far from harmless. He was a shark, but that combination of brains and instinct was like an irresistible pheromone that few could resist.

Even me?

"He certainly is." She smiled, knowing she looked cool and unconcerned, and no one could tell that sweat had started to bead between her breasts. She could resist the irresistible. She had to.

"He's going to be tough competition for you." Was Elise fishing for the inside scoop, curious to see if there was more than just a friendly business rivalry between them? Or was Liz projecting her own feelings and fears onto others?

She shook it off and grinned. "Oh, I think maybe it's going to be the other way around."

Elise smiled back at her. "That's a great attitude to have. We should definitely talk some more. I'll see you later at your pitch."

"That sounds perfect." Liz took the woman's card. With a wave good-bye, she turned around and walked right into a man who'd been crossing behind her.

"I'm so sorry," she said, brushing the lapel of his jacket. She'd managed to hold onto her coffee cup. Thankfully, it was almost empty, and she'd opted for the plastic lid, or else what was left of it would have landed all over his beautiful charcoal gray suit. "It's crazy in here, but I should be more careful, especially with coffee in my hand." She looked up into a pair of the deepest brown eyes she'd ever seen.

"So you're Elizabeth Carlson." His voice was low with a hint of appreciation, but his smile was light and friendly.

"I am." She straightened her suit jacket and glanced down at the name badge hanging around her neck, but it had swung around so he couldn't have seen it.

She readjusted the plastic sleeve and held out her free hand. "I'm sorry, how do we know each other?"

His big hand swallowed hers up in a firm grip. "Oh, we don't. Not formally anyway, but I have to tell you…" He leaned in a little bit, voice dropping to a whisper. "You look fantastic in a red bikini."

She gasped and tugged her hand away, frowning up at his still smiling face. "I don't think…"

He chuckled. "My apologies, I shouldn't have teased you."

"Then why did you?"

He laughed. "I guess I already feel as if we know each other. I'm Stephen Nolan. You obviously didn't notice me the other day at the pool."

Ben Harrison's right-hand man. The magazines featured Nolan even more often than his partner. While Ben might have been granted a kind of celebrity status by stepping out with Meredith Stone, apparently Nolan was a celebrity in his own right. He was some kind of financial genius who'd gotten into NYU on a football scholarship and ended up surprising everyone with the fact that he also had a brain.

There'd been a time when those good looks and brainpower had been nothing compared to the money and social influence of his family, but from what she'd read, the only thing left of the Nolan dynasty was probably a closet full of those perfectly cut suits.

As he stood before her, there was a stiffness in his shoulders that went all the way up to his eyes. It made his easy, flirty smile look like a mask that didn't quite fit. Maybe it had at one time, but she got the impression this guy had been pretending to be a lot of things to a lot of people, and maybe nobody knew the deep down and dirty person who really lived in his skin.

Liz held out her hand again. "Let's do that again without the reference to my bikini, okay?"

He laughed. "Of course, how unprofessional of me."

She quirked an eyebrow. "I have a feeling you go out of your way to be unprofessional a lot of the time, don't you?"

His expression was finally loosening up a little. His grin looked real, like he was actually having fun with her now instead of just pretending. "Well, now that you mention it…"

She shook her finger. "Just be sure it doesn't bite you in the ass and get you in trouble one of these days."

"Great advice, and I suppose I should hope it's not already too late, shouldn't I?" With a sideways grin, he reached out to shake her hand again. "So Ms. Carlson, let me re-introduce myself. I'm Stephen Nolan of Optimus Inc. It's lovely to meet you in person. I've heard quite a bit about you in the last few days from my partner."

She laughed. "It's very…interesting to meet you as well, Mr. Nolan, but please don't tell me what you've heard from Ben."

"All good things," he assured her. "Maybe a little intimidating, actually. In fact, faced with such indomitable competition, I think Harrison and I are going to have to step up our game."

She somehow doubted that the two dynamic men who made up Optimus Inc. were going to have any trouble getting their fair share of the attention during this convention. Leaving aside issues of product superiority, their reputations alone were sure to guarantee success.

Ben and his partner had had their pictures in the magazines. Each of them looked damn amazing in a suit, oozed confidence and charisma, and could charm the pants off a room full of conference attendees. She needed to charm these same people if she was going to win their vote at the end of this week and win Tyson Wallace's endorsement.

It was intimidating, to say the least, but men had been trying to intimidate her since she'd written her first line of code back in high school—and done it quicker and better than the male students sitting beside her. This business was all about results, and she knew she could deliver. When it came down to doing some real business, Diego Vargas wasn't going to be looking at who was more popular. He would want to invest in the company that had the best chance of making him money, and Sharkston Co. had every bit the same chance of being that company as Optimus Inc.

"Please call me Liz," she said with a smile. "And in the spirit of healthy competition, let me wish you good luck as the convention gets underway."

"Good luck to you, too."

"Speaking of competition," he said as she was turning to go. "I might be stepping out of line here—"

"And that's different from two minutes ago because…?"

He chuckled and dipped his head in acknowledgement of her point. "Ben and I have a friend in common, Meredith Stone, who happens to be my roommate at the convention."

"Your…?"

She blushed as it became clear what he was getting at, probably thinking Liz cared who Ben was or wasn't seeing.

Okay, so maybe she did care.

Setting that aside, she was obviously naïve enough to hope that Ben wasn't sleeping with Meredith Stone… but was she really supposed to believe that Nolan wasn't sleeping with her either? That they were only *roommates*?

He must have seen her skepticism. "The three of us have a complicated relationship."

"It's fine. You don't have to say anything. It's really none of my business." So it was like *that*? She waved her hand and took a step back.

Right into yet another hard body.

"Oh, not again. I'm so sorry. I'm such a klutz today." Instinctively, she smacked her hand over the lid of her coffee cup.

"Just what is this guy telling you?"

Ben.

As she turned and saw that Meredith Stone was standing right there beside him, she fumbled. Her heel caught in the fiber of the carpeting, and she lost her balance.

He quickly reached out to steady her. Such a simple and innocent thing, but from him it totally wasn't. She glanced around to see who might have been watching. Were the undercurrents running between them as obvious to everyone else? Something so strong couldn't go completely unnoticed, right?

His arm fell away almost immediately, and she felt both relief and an odd shimmer of excitement. The hint of secrecy and touch of the forbidden sent adrenaline rushing through her system.

When she glanced up, he looked calm and easy, but there was a twinkle in his eyes that was all too knowing and threatened to make her blush.

Liz brushed invisible wrinkles from her jacket and struggled to find something casual to say, afraid that anything that came out of her mouth would expose her feelings, reveal the sad fact that she was becoming more vulnerable every time she saw him.

So she looked away to try and catch her breath, only to find Meredith Stone watching her with a hard look in her eyes. "Ms. Stone," she said, shaky. "I've seen you in the magazines, haven't I? Mr. Nolan here was just telling me how very…close…the three of you are."

Ben gave Steve a dark look. "He was, was he?"

"I think I might have given Ms. Carlson the wrong impression about our friendship," Steve said with a chuckle. "Like maybe there's some kind of decadent threesome going on between all of us."

Liz choked and looked back and forth between the two men, even as her heart plummeted. "It's none of my business."

Meredith planted her perfectly manicured hands on her hips and glared at Nolan. "You really can't be trusted in polite company, can you?" she said.

Steve glanced over their shoulders and suddenly tensed. "You're absolutely right. I'll leave it in your capable hands to clear up this misunderstanding." He turned to Liz. "I look forward to pitting Optimus Inc. against Sharkston Co."

From anyone else, she might have thought he was being insolent, but the respect and warmth in his tone made it obvious he considered her a serious rival. At the same time, he seemed to be able to take the whole thing the way it was meant to be taken—as good-natured competition.

Steve turned and made a beeline for the other end of the registration room. She lost sight of him just as a tall blond woman stopped in front of her and Ben. "Excuse me, the man you were just speaking with, Stephen Nolan, did he say where he was going?"

Meredith frowned. "Why? Who are you?" she said bluntly. "Was he expecting you? Do you have business with him?"

The woman focused her attention on Ben with a practiced smile and flipped her hair before snapping her hand out for his. "I'm Veronica Ash with the *Times*," she said. "I'd just like to get a quote for our article. You're his partner, aren't you? Benjamin Harrison?"

The woman ignored Meredith and hadn't even registered Liz's presence. Ben shook her hand. "It's nice to meet you, but perhaps we can arrange something later?" he said. "I have a few meetings this morning, and I still have to pick up my registration package."

The woman twined her fingers together in front of her, but her voice was high and bright as she responded, "Oh of course, I'll catch you later. Thanks for your time."

Liz chuckled. "More interviews of the playboy genius?"

Ben threw a glance back over his shoulder and grinned. "I have a feeling she was more interested in the free trip to Antigua than the idea of covering a boring tech convention."

"Your partner didn't strike me as the shy type, but he seemed pretty eager to avoid her."

Ben nodded. "Given his history, Nolan has limited patience with the press. He'll probably go hide out at the poker game downstairs whenever he can."

Liz froze in her tracks, dread hitting her like a Mack truck. "There's a poker game going on at the resort?"

Ben turned and stopped in front of her. "It's a private, invitation-only, high stakes game that goes on in the lounge pretty much twenty-four hours a day. They keep it quiet for the most part, but I've heard that a few people have been playing."

"Have you played?" she asked. If so, had he seen Daniel there? Is that why her brother had been scarce lately?

"No, of course not. You know gambling isn't my thing. Why do you ask?"

"No reason." She prayed he would let it go.

"All right then, let's go find our conference room."

It would have been too much to hope that Meredith and Ben weren't planning to sit in on her pitch session, but she could handle it. Ben Harrison would *not* make her nervous.

She nodded and marched ahead, refusing to let him lead the way.

Was that him chuckling behind her? She glanced over her shoulder. His eyes sparkled with devilment. Yep, either that, or he'd been staring at her ass.

Maybe both.

When they arrived, she was actually glad Ben stood with

her. The place was already packed with people, all of whom turned to look as the two of them entered. Their appearance together gave the impression—not exactly false—that this rivalry was all in good fun.

She took a deep breath.

"You're going to knock 'em dead," Ben said in her ear.

"I think I'm a little nervous," she admitted with a shaky laugh.

"Well, you've got two options," he said. "One, you just don't think about the audience, and instead you get up there and talk about your work like you're explaining it to your best friend."

She turned back to him. "Why would I do that?"

"Because there's no pressure talking to a friend, and all the excitement and enthusiasm for what you love to do will come out and be obvious to everyone here. That's really what they all want to see, anyway."

She was surprised he was giving her such honest advice in this moment when they were supposed to be at their most competitive, but she smiled and nodded, because he was absolutely right.

"What's the other option?"

He grinned. "You imagine everyone in the audience naked."

She groaned and shook her head. "I should have known you were going to come up with that."

Since he would be up next right after her, she held out her hand. "Good luck to you," she said. His big, warm hand closed over hers with a shocking zap, and suddenly it was all she could do to shake it casually and turn away.

She locked down her nerves and looked for Daniel.

Thank God, he was already at the front of the room, and—*Oh. My. God.*—he was talking with Diego Vargas who was sitting front and center, with an arm thrown comfortably across the back of the empty chair beside him.

Ben followed her down the aisle to the front of the room. It would probably be rude if she told him to leave, but he could have at least stayed in the back where she wouldn't be able to see him, couldn't he? She decided to just ignore him.

She said hello to Vargas and shook his hand, even though her palm still bore the heat of Ben's touch. "I didn't think I would see you here this morning, Mr. Vargas."

"It's just Diego, remember?" He straightened when he saw Ben. "I know I've already gotten the early intro to both Optimus Inc. and Sharkston Co., and what you're all about, but I couldn't resist seeing what you both can do in front of a group of people."

She and Ben both laughed. "So the pressure's on, is it?" she said.

He grinned. "If you want to look at it that way."

"All right then, we had better get started. Excuse me."

She and Daniel quickly finished setting up the visuals for their presentation. A moment later, Laura took the podium. She smiled broadly at Daniel and gave Liz a friendly wink before turning to the audience.

"Before I introduce our guests this morning, I want to remind you of the competition we have going on this year, and the ballot box sitting on the table outside the large conference room," she said. "Don't forget to cast your votes for one of these dynamic companies before the closing luncheon. The winner of Tyson Wallace's endorsement will be named at that time."

Liz breathed deeply as she waited for the crowd to quiet down. Ben had taken the extra seat beside Diego and smiled up at her, but if he intended his presence to throw her off, he would be disappointed. Having him there was surprisingly reassuring. He was a familiar face, and as she got started, that made it easier to take his advice and speak as if she were talking to a friend—because she *did* have a friend in the audience.

Daniel spoke about matters of Sharkston's corporate structure, and she fielded everything related to their product design and technology. Their thirty minutes was over before she knew it, and Laura gave the audience another fifteen minutes to ask questions, which Liz and her brother fielded easily enough. She was feeling really good about everything, but part of her expected Ben to pipe up with questions designed to undermine her company.

He didn't say anything at all.

There were still hands in the air, and although Laura hadn't stepped forward yet to put a stop to the discussion, Liz wanted to be fair to Ben. "Thank you for your rapt attention this morning," she said. "So that we don't intrude on Mr. Harrison and Mr. Nolan's time now, I'm more than happy to answer any more questions after Optimus Inc.'s presentation."

The audience clapped politely as she and Daniel stepped down. She followed him to the back of the room, but when he went to open the door and leave, she grabbed his arm. "Aren't you going to stay and see how Ben and his partner do?"

He glanced back and shook his head. "Naw, it doesn't matter."

"How can you say that?" she whispered.

He raised a brow. "You're going to stay, aren't you?"

"Well, yes but…"

"Then you can fill me in later, right?"

"I suppose. You have somewhere else you need to be?"

"It's no big deal. If you want me to stay, I'll stay." Resentment clouded his voice. She shook her head.

"No, you're right. I guess there's no reason why we both have to stay. You go. I'll catch up with you later."

He left without another word, and Liz leaned against the back wall to watch Ben and Nolan, but she couldn't shake the hollow feeling in the pit of her stomach. As the discussion got started, though, her attention was diverted.

She realized Ben was staring over everyone's heads, right at her. Was he taking his own advice? Talking about Optimus Inc. as if it was just the two of them? Two friends?

She caught the gleam in his eyes. No, he was using that other common strategy for speaking to large groups… imagining the crowd naked.

Imagining *her* naked.

A hot blush spread across her face, and she squeezed her eyes shut to escape that potent gaze…but then it was just her and his voice. His equally potent, confident, deep voice burrowing into her head until she was picturing them *both* naked…and sweaty…and—

She was suddenly very glad that she'd already finished her presentation. She opened her eyes. Nobody was looking at her anymore anyway, so who cared if she was blushing?

Before long, she was completely drawn into the discussion. Ben's easy demeanor and conversational style made it easy. She was even able to forget that in his head she was probably still moonlighting without her clothes.

He was a natural in front of the audience. She was pretty sure she'd been able to mask most of her nerves, but there was no way he even *had* any.

When the presentation was finished, it was impossible to tell which way the audience was leaning. She stood back and tried to compartmentalize what she'd learned about Optimus Inc. this morning with what she'd already surmised from her research. There were many similarities in the technologies the two companies were developing, but what would really set them apart were the business platforms each of them had developed. She was eager to sit down later with Daniel and adjust their strategy based on this morning's presentations.

That made her wonder just where he had been going earlier. Was the lure of a poker game so compelling that he was no longer able to focus on his job?

She noticed Meredith Stone. The woman came forward. "I was impressed with your presentation, Ms. Carlson."

"Thank you. Please, just call me Liz."

The room had started to empty, and Ben approached.

Meredith smiled up at him, looking sweet and alluring, femininely confident and intriguingly mysterious, all at the same time. Liz had never been even half of those things in her entire life. "You did a fantastic job," Meredith said, touching his shoulder. Liz swallowed and pretended not to notice.

Ben grinned and turned to Liz. "Would you like to hang back, and we can discuss our plans for the workshop?"

She wrung her hands together, worried. "Do you mind if we postpone that for a little while? I've just remembered there's something I need to do now."

He frowned. "Sure, but we'll have to get our ducks in a

row as soon as we can. The workshop is tomorrow morning."

"I know, I just—"

"Beth, talk to me. What is it? What happened? Is this about the poker game? Is your brother still getting into that kind of trouble? Is there anything I can do to help?"

He looked concerned, and she hated that he knew her family history, worse that he'd mentioned it in front of someone like Meredith. It made her feel vulnerable, but she tried to tell herself he would never use it against her.

She worked on settling her nerves and finally shook her head. She had to trust her brother. If she didn't give him the benefit of the doubt, she'd end up undermining all the hard work he'd put in to overcome his gambling problems.

"No, Daniel's fine. Never mind. It's nothing, and you're right, we should get this seminar planned out. Just let me stop by the registration desk first." She looked at Meredith. "If you'll excuse me."

"Let me join you," said Ben. "Mer, are you hanging out poolside today?"

"That's the plan, but we'll have to see how the weather holds up. Maybe I'll get lucky and find Mr. Perfect out there, but feel free to come get me for lunch, if you're not too busy."

She turned to Liz and gave her a surprisingly stern once-over. Finally, she leaned in close to whisper in her ear. "Be gentle with him, Ms. Carlson. He's a good friend, and I'd hate to see him bruised a second time by the likes of you."

Startled by the warning, Liz jerked her gaze to Ben, who looked on with a frown creasing his forehead. But Meredith was already sauntering away.

"Was that something I should know about?"

"No, I…" She shook her head, at a loss. Was it true? Had

she actually *hurt* Ben? She'd never really thought about it that way. She supposed she'd just believed that his proposal had been more about their work, and by kissing her, Ben had kind of thrown that other thing out there as a "what if." When she shot it down for obvious reasons, he'd just shrugged it off and continued on his way…at least that's exactly what he'd seemed to do. "It was nothing."

Twenty minutes later, she sat at a conference table and flipped open her notebook, trying very hard not to notice the way his body moved as he took off his suit jacket and placed it over the back of a chair.

"What are you thinking about?" he asked, taking a chair right beside her instead of sitting across the table.

She nervously tapped her pen to the page. "What? Why?"

"I remember that look. It's the coding look. You're trying to figure something out, solve a puzzle." He smiled and lifted his finger to trace the furrow in her brow. "So, what is it?"

"What's the real deal between you and Meredith?" She regretted asking as soon as the words passed her lips and shook her head. "Never mind. I wasn't going to…it's really none of my…"

"No, it's fine." He sat back in his chair. "I should have laid that out before now."

"So, is she or isn't she your girlfriend? Or Steve's girlfriend?" She raised an eyebrow. "Or…both?"

"Neither," he said. "Really."

"Because it just looked…I mean, she's really gorgeous, and all of you seem really close. She's the one who dragged you to Antigua before, isn't she? And I…we…I just don't want to get in the middle of something."

He leaned in toward her, bracing his elbows on his knees. "*You're* really gorgeous, you know that?"

"Ben, be serious," she said. "You do know how to do that, right?"

"Yes, I know how to do that." He was so close to her now she could see the flecks of cobalt in his deep blue eyes. "Meredith is a friend. We tried the dating thing for a while—hence all the magazine photos—but it was apparent very quickly that I wasn't really her type."

"Why not?"

He chuckled. "You sound offended on my behalf. I'm flattered."

She smacked him in the shoulder. "Just keep talking."

With a cheeky grin, he grabbed his arm like she'd fatally wounded him, but then he sobered and said, "I was supremely uncomfortable with all the society events. It's a whole other life that Meredith has a place in, but we couldn't quite find a way for me to fit into it."

"Were you not pretentious and boring enough?"

"How did you know? Wait, don't tell Meredith I said that." He laughed.

"From the day we met, you showed an interest in two things: coding and reckless escapades, and I have a feeling that neither of those goes well with tuxedos, golf, and orchestra music."

"Truthfully, she's a wonderful person. She was there for me when Olsen killed himself, and we've become really good friends."

"I noticed that." She tried not to sound jealous. It wasn't jealousy she felt. She didn't know what it was exactly. Hell, maybe it *was* jealousy. Not because she was worried that he had a thing for the woman…maybe she was jealous that he'd found friendships in New York that meant as much to him as their friendship had meant once.

"So now she's with Steve?"

"Ah, no. Also just a friend," he said with a smile.

"Oh, I thought because she came here with him…"

"She came because it was an opportunity to avoid her father at home for a few days. They don't exactly get along."

"Oh," Liz still didn't understand. "I assume she's still living at home then, but why? If Meredith and her father don't get along, why doesn't she move into her own place?"

"She can't. Not if she wants to claim her inheritance next year." Ben shrugged. "It's one of those complicated family situations involving generations of people with roman numerals after their names."

He leaned back in his chair again and crossed his arms. "Was there something else you wanted to get out in the open?"

Was that a dare? Maybe she should tell him that she regretted her decision that day when he kissed her for the first time, and that she was probably falling in love with him now? That she was starting to think she'd always been in love with him, and that's why she had shoved him away? She'd never meant to hurt him, and the thought of it made her feel like she was drowning.

She took a sip of her fresh cup of coffee and squared her shoulders. She needed to refocus on the real reason she was in Antigua.

"Okay, so I've gone over the current convention schedule, and I don't think we can pull off the same topic Tyson Wallace would have presented. But given our areas of expertise, it looks like we can fill the gap with domain-specific superintelligences, or maybe initial motivations and conditions." She glanced up to find him listening intently. "Unless you think an ethics discussion is too heavy for an event like this."

"No, I agree. With the AI systems we've both specialized in, ethics is an important component of that. I think the audience will be curious to learn how two separate companies have treated a similar issue."

"Oh, good. I'm glad we're on the same page."

A while later, they had come up with an outline for the seminar, but also left some unstructured time in the schedule. Ben had seemed to think they should leave even more time for a question and answer session, believing that the audience would be engaged in the discussion. But Liz wanted to make sure they had enough material to cover the entire time slot, just in case the room was quiet. She flipped back over the pages of notes they'd made when it occurred to her they had missed something.

"What about the closing speech?" she asked.

Ben leaned back in his chair and crossed his arms, looking at her until she shifted in her seat.

"What is it?" She glanced down at her shirt. "Did I spill my coffee?"

"This is…nice," he said in a low voice. "We make a good team."

With a laugh she said, "Sure. As long as it only involves planning an hour-long discussion for a bunch of convention guests."

"You don't think we could take this kind of cooperation to the next level?"

Her pulse raced at the implication. She put her pen

down carefully. "You might have moved to New York to start your business, but this industry is still a small world, and I've heard all about how you operate. You're a ruthless and uncompromising businessman, and I could never have been your partner."

His gaze narrowed. "This is about what I told you yesterday? About Olsen?"

"No, of course not," she said quickly. "But you can't deny that we could never have worked together like this for real. I didn't start my business to become rich, and I don't need to always be the best," she said.

He pulled back, looking practically insulted. "Then what's the point of doing it at all?"

"That's *exactly* my point," she said, trying not to be insulted in return by his arrogance. "We have completely different ways of looking at our futures. I got into programming because I love it, because it's something I'm good at, and because it challenges me, and I started my business because that way I can keep doing what I love on my own schedule. But I want a real life, too. It's one thing to devote all my energy to the work now, while I don't have anything more important in my life, or—"

"What else could be more important? And if you just want to fool around, why would you even bother seeking investment capital?"

She gritted her teeth. He wasn't getting it. "I may not need to be the best, but that doesn't mean I'm not the best," she answered with a confident grin. "I'm proud of my work, and I want to use it to build a good life for the family I might have in the future."

"How is that any different from what I wanted for the

two of us?"

"You forget how well I know you, Ben. Your drive to succeed always felt more like a hell-bent determination to prove something." She bit her lip, trying to decide how to explain. "Maybe to the father who thought he was too good for you?"

His jaw snapped shut like a steel trap, and a tangible barrier went up between them that felt like ice. She'd gone too far. Should never have mentioned his father. "I...I'm sorry," she stammered. "I only meant that—"

He nodded, but the tight frown on his face only deepened. "It's okay. You're right. I went to New York with every intention of doing whatever it took to get my company off the ground. I would never have let anything or anyone stand in my way, not even you. And you would have tried, because you're too nice to do business with someone like me. But sometimes you have to be ruthless to get what you want."

"But there are different ways to approach it. There's always a way—"

"Don't be naïve. I never would have survived in this industry if I didn't cut Olsen loose."

"What if Steve had done the same to you?"

"He almost did, and he would have had every right."

"What do you mean?"

"I was a control freak."

"No...not *you*?" She faked a laugh, because she was biting back tears and couldn't bear to let him see.

"When I brought Steve Nolan on board as my partner," he continued, "I thought I could continue to make all the decisions just the way I always had, but after the third time

I tried to railroad something past him, he up and quit. When I followed him to his boxing club and demanded to know what the hell he thought he was doing, he called me up onto the mats and set me straight, at the same time that he beat the crap out of me."

A bittersweet smile pulled at her lips. "I think I would have liked to see that."

His lips twisted. "*Everyone* liked to see that."

She got to her feet and took a step toward him. "Jeffrey Olsen was just a man," she said in a soft voice. "A tired, defeated man whose last lifeline was ripped from his grasp just when he needed it the most."

His expression tightened. "So you *do* think I killed him."

"No! Oh Ben, that's not what I was trying to say at all."

"But it's what you think." He stepped away. "I suppose it's a good thing you refused to come to New York with me. I wouldn't have wanted you to get your hands dirty—"

She gasped. "That's not fair."

His lips pressed together in a tight expression. "No, it's not. I'm sorry."

"Wait, where are you going?"

"We're done here, so I'm going to go." He was already halfway out of the room by the time she caught up.

He kept going as if he couldn't get away from her fast enough, with long strides that made her feel guiltier with every step.

Liz's shoulders drooped. She'd handled that so horribly. Ben had always been driven to succeed, but she'd known him all through college right up until the day he left for New York, and he had never been cruel or unfair to anyone. Not like she'd just been to him.

She needed to find a way to apologize, but first she wanted to talk to Daniel. She hadn't seen much of him. After exiting the elevator on his floor, she walked down the hall and knocked at his door. "Daniel?" She knocked again, but there was still no answer.

Maybe he'd gone down to the restaurant for lunch… maybe with the woman he'd hinted at meeting yesterday. She turned and walked a few steps back down the hall.

The door opened behind her, and she turned around again. Daniel leaned out into the hall. He looked tired and mussed. What the hell happened since she saw him this morning? Her heart leaped into her throat. "Hey, there you are," she said.

"Yeah Liz, here I am," he said around a mouthful. "What do you need?"

He was shoveling down a bagel like the world might end if he didn't get it all into his mouth in time. She forced a chuckle. "Is this the first time you've eaten since landing on the island or something?"

He paused with his hand halfway to his mouth and swallowed. "I skipped breakfast and didn't have much for dinner last night," he mumbled.

"Didn't you go on a date? How did it go?" Did he not even get through dinner with this woman?

"It was great." He grinned and crossed his arms as the last bite of bagel went down the hatch. "What, do you want details or something?"

"Hell no." She shook her head and shuddered at the thought. "I'm just happy you had a good time. Um…I think that's what I feel. It could be something else, though. Like mild disgust."

He laughed then straightened from the doorjamb. "Now you know how I feel about you hanging out with Harrison. How did that go, anyway? Did you at least get something we can use against him in our negotiations with Diego Vargas?"

"Let's not start playing dirty. If we have respect for our competitors, they'll have respect for us. Besides, Ben has had enough trouble with—" She shut her mouth.

He scowled. "With what? What's that supposed to mean?"

She shook her head. "Never mind. I shouldn't have mentioned anything."

"If it's something that could help us—"

"Just drop it, Daniel. We're not using it against him. It wouldn't be professional."

The way he looked at her, she thought he was going to keep pushing, but he finally said, "Whatever. Listen, I should probably take a shower and get dressed, so I'll talk to you later okay?"

She let out a relieved sigh. "Do you want to get together for lunch, and we can go over some details for the next two days?"

"Well, if you need me, sure…but I made tentative plans to meet Laura again for lunch," he said shyly.

"Her name is Laura? Wouldn't happen to be the same Laura from the convention committee, would it?"

"Yeah, actually. She called me yesterday morning looking for you."

"I remember you mentioned it. So how did you two get together?"

"Well, we kind of ran into each other yesterday afternoon and it just kind of…" Was that a blush crawling up his neck? He shrugged, and Liz grinned.

She was more relieved than she'd ever admit out loud to hear that her brother had been ditching his job duties for a girl. It was much better than wondering if he'd been sitting at a table somewhere gambling again.

"Don't worry about it. We don't really need to do much this afternoon anyway."

"Are you sure?"

She smiled and waved it off. "Yeah, of course. You haven't had a vacation in as long as I have…and I haven't had one like, ever, so you should get a chance to enjoy yourself. I've already done some brainstorming with Ben for the seminar, and I can handle the networking this afternoon. Why don't I give you a call later?"

"Okay, thanks." He looked relieved, too, as if he'd expected her to crack down on him.

She gave him a hug and said good-bye, but as she turned to go and Daniel started to close the door, she caught a glimpse of another expression that brought back every bit of her worry and uncertainty.

Guilt.

Chapter Eleven

With the convention in full swing, the lobby, restaurant, and other common areas were full of people. Some of them Ben recognized, but many he didn't. If Optimus Inc. was going to win the vote and be honored with Tyson Wallace's endorsement, he and Nolan needed to be aggressive and make their presence known.

Much like Beth had been doing this evening.

She always seemed to be on the other side of the bar, but his gaze found her easily. She smiled, working the room just as determinedly as they were, bravely talking to all the heavy-hitting execs from the big companies…and doing a great job from the looks of it. She was absolutely stunning in a sleek dress that was not quite red, but not pink either, managing to look both sexy and professional at the same time. Confidence and enthusiasm shone from her face. He'd been catching snippets of conversation, and it seemed that comparisons between Optimus Inc. and Sharkston Co. were the hot topic. He couldn't have gotten better publicity this week if he'd paid for it.

"He's ours," said Nolan, talking about Diego Vargas. He seemed to think that after the presentations this morning, Optimus was nosing ahead in the competition. He lifted his half-empty glass of draught with a grin. "The only thing left to do now is close the deal."

"Not so fast," said Ben. He was confident too, but knew he couldn't afford to get cocky, and he was surprisingly torn between wanting to win—needing to win—and wanting to see Beth succeed.

Nolan nudged him in the arm. "Shouldn't you be more impressed with yourself right now?"

"I just don't think we should be counting the money until it's actually in our account."

"Come on, he loves us." They'd spent happy hour in the bar with Vargas, who had just left to get ready for a dinner meeting. "As long as we can get him committed to at least a handshake deal, we'll be set."

Ben didn't disagree. Vargas had been totally on board with their pitch from start to finish. He'd asked insightful questions and seemed interested in seeing and hearing more as soon as it could be arranged. The only hiccup had been his obvious interest in Beth's product as well, but Ben knew that he could swing things his way if he really wanted to. All it would take was a few subtle insinuations about the unreliability of Sharkston Co.'s other partner and his penchant for gambling, and nobody would want to take that kind of risk.

He grimaced, disgusted that the thought had even crossed his mind.

"And as long as you continue the great job you're doing keeping the competition occupied—"

"What is that supposed to mean?"

"You don't have to play dumb with me, I'm totally on board with whatever game you want to play."

"I'm not playing games with Beth." Wasn't he, though? What were they doing if not playing games? It wasn't as if he thought they had something serious, something that could last after they both left this island.

And even if he was somehow stupid enough to think they did, after their conversation this morning, Beth obviously had no such delusions.

"Okay, sure. Whatever you say as long as we get the investment we need from Vargas," said Nolan.

"I have a feeling he'll hold his decision close to the chest until after the vote at the end of the week." He crossed his arms. "Shouldn't you go find Meredith and make sure she's staying out of trouble?"

With a grimace, Nolan drained his glass. "All she did today was complain about the weather. How was I supposed to know we'd land in Antigua just in time for a tropical storm?"

The storm was still just a prediction, but the sun hadn't made much of an appearance today. "I think the convention organizers planned it this way so we'll all be good little industry professionals and attend their carefully planned sessions instead of heading for the beach."

Not that Ben had noticed the weather at all. He hadn't stepped foot out of doors all day. Then again, he'd been outside all day yesterday and still hadn't noticed anything except for Beth. A hurricane could have been raging around him, and he would only have seen her smile.

"And here I was, counting on everyone to leave the resort and take advantage of the sunshine so that I could get some work done without looking over my shoulder the whole time," said Nolan.

"Does that mean you're ready to tell me what the hell is going on, and why you need a buffer between you and some reporter?" Ben asked his friend.

"Okay, I admit it. I'm trying to hide from the woman from the *Times*. No matter where I go or what I do, I can't seem to shake her."

It was a running joke that Steve had a horde of women stalking him, but this time he wasn't laughing about it. "Is there something going on between the two of you?"

"Jesus, no," he said quickly. Too quickly?

"*Was* there something going on between you?" he amended.

Nolan groaned. "Nothing serious. We had a little fun, that's all."

"And did she *know* it was nothing serious?"

"Yeah, of course. You know me."

The trouble was, Ben did know him. And while his friend never went into anything without being completely honest, he was also the type of guy women thought they could "change."

But it was none of his business. If Steve couldn't handle it, he'd say something when he was good and ready. Ben checked the time and stood to retrieve his jacket from the back of the chair. "Are we still meeting the rep from Magnatech later?"

"I can take care of it." Nolan threw him a knowing look.

"Don't you have some more work to do with Ms. Carlson before your seminar tomorrow?"

Ben glanced at her again. She was smiling and shaking hands with the CEO from Innotech, who Ben and Nolan had already met with earlier. He shrugged.

"Exactly what is the deal with the two of you?"

He lifted an eyebrow. "Are you sure nothing else is going on between you and the reporter that I should know about?"

Nolan raised his hands in the air. "Never mind. Forget I asked."

...

Liz left the bar after making the rounds during happy hour. Daniel hadn't answered his cell all afternoon, so she stopped by his room to see if he wanted to go down to dinner. There was no answer at the door. Convincing herself he was with Laura and not playing poker was easier this time, and she went back to her own room instead of going to dinner alone. It would be a good night to hunker down and get some work done.

She was certain she wouldn't be able to concentrate, but when there was a knock at the door three hours later, she looked up in surprise. With a stretch, she put aside her laptop and uncurled herself from the bed.

She half expected it to be Daniel, checking in on her, but Ben stood in the doorway. She couldn't help giving him the once-over, even though she'd been eyeing him earlier in the bar every chance she got. He looked absolutely fantastic in a navy suit and bright green striped tie.

She looked down at her boxer shorts and tank top and crossed her arms. She was *so* not prepared for him right now.

"Hi. I didn't see you downstairs for dinner, so I took a chance you might be up here," he said, hands stuffed in his pockets. "I thought maybe we should talk."

Feeling unaccountably nervous, she smiled stupidly and motioned for him to come in. "I'm actually glad you're here. I've felt horrible about what I said to you this morning, and I need to apologize. I never meant—"

"Stop," he interrupted her. "I'm the one who should explain."

"No really, I never believed for a second that Jeffrey Olsen's death was in any way your fault."

"I know you didn't—"

"And you're absolutely right. Every industry is competitive, and this one can be absolutely brutal. You have to be a shark to succeed, and you can't be responsible for the ways in which other people handle their failures." She shook her head. "I had no right—"

She hadn't realized she'd started pacing in front of him until he grabbed her wrist and pulled her up short. His touch started an immediate chain reaction of quivering sensation all the way to her toes, and she froze. Breathless, she looked up.

"Beth, it's okay," he said in a low voice. "I shouldn't have walked away."

She cocked her head. "Why did you?"

He sighed, touching his thumb to the center of her palm as if it was a subconscious impulse like when she flipped her hair back behind her ear...or paced the floor. His thumb rubbed drugging circles into her arm. "Seeing you again these last few days has reminded me of some things I lost—or forgot—when I went to New York."

"Like what?" She drifted closer until she had to look up to maintain eye contact.

"Like the kind of man I used to be, the kind I want to be again. I used to love the simplicity of that spark of discovery in every code. Every day was a new adventure. But when you rejected me, that changed a little bit. Then Olsen happened, and I had to re-think everything. What you said earlier was no surprise. I've known for a long time that if you'd come to New York, I would have destroyed everything about you that I love. The purity of your gift, your love for the job… what we had together."

"Oh Ben," she whispered, undone by his honesty and vulnerability and surprised that he seemed to trust her enough to see it.

She trailed a finger along the shadowed line of his jaw, the scratchiness giving her shivers as she imagined how it would leave red marks all over her skin when he kissed her breasts, her belly, and between her thighs…

"I've missed you more than I even realized. We were such close friends and then…we weren't, and I didn't want to admit that I was the one who destroyed it," she said. "I blamed you for rocking the boat, but it was me. I was the one who let my fears get in the way of something that might have been even better than friendship."

He leaned down, a dark challenge shadowing his deep blue eyes. "Is that what we are?"

The same words he'd used earlier when she had talked about being enemies. "What? Friends?"

"No…" he said with a smoking look, making it obvious

that he remembered their earlier exchange just as well as she did. He pulled her hard against him. "*Close*."

After what he'd just told her, she had to be as honest as he'd been. "I'm torn between wanting you so much it's penetrated every part of my body like a fever," she said with a groan as her arms climbed his chest to his shoulders. "And needing my friend back, because I've missed what we had, missed the way we were before everything changed."

"It's too late. We can't go back and reclaim what we had before," he murmured against her skin, his lips already doing their damnedest to mark her as his with hot, open-mouthed kisses pressed to the spot under her ear and down the length of her nape. "But I'm a firm believer in seizing the moment that's right in front of us here and now."

"Ah, yes. A *firm*, um, believer. Oh God." Her head fell back, and he dipped his tongue into the hollow of her throat where her pulse beat fast.

It was so hard to think, to form the words she should have said that very first time he'd kissed her. The words that would betray just how much he'd meant to her then and now, and how much fear those feelings engendered within her. She'd let fear get the better of her then. In trying to preserve what they had, she'd lost the very thing she'd valued the most.

So maybe it was best that she couldn't speak, because she didn't want to make the same mistake again.

When they finally took a breath, every sense she had was bloated with him. The feel of him, the scent of him, the rhythmic thumping of his heart against her chest. It was more than she could handle, and she needed a moment to try thinking about what was happening without the overwhelming influence of her physical desire clouding the matter.

She pulled away and hugged herself tight, desperately trying to focus on something besides Ben, but the only thing to catch her attention was the massive king-sized bed waiting for them in the middle of the room. "I have to...I'll be right back."

Like a coward, she retreated to the bathroom. The bright light blinded her, and she blinked into the mirror. "What am I doing?" she whispered.

When they were friends, they'd been friends, and the expectations of that relationship had been well defined. Then they weren't friends, and he was gone, and she'd eventually gotten used to that too. Even when she'd contemplated having an island fling, she'd conceived of very distinct rules for how it should proceed.

But it wasn't working out that way. Ben wasn't sticking within her pre-drawn boundary lines. He was destroying all of her neat little boxes as if they were wobbly sand castles leaning toward the beach, and he was the tide crashing in over them all.

She took a deep breath and squared her shoulders before absently washing her hands so maybe he wouldn't guess that she'd run to hide.

When she came back out, he was standing by the bed near her computer. "Have you eaten?" he asked.

She paused, taken off guard by the unexpected question. "Now that you mention it, I kind of skipped dinner. I got busy with work, and it didn't seem like much of a priority."

He picked up the phone on the nightstand and dialed. "Hello, this is Benjamin Harrison. Are you still serving dinner in the kitchen? Good. Charge my account, but bring up two of your specials to room 304. And a bottle of the Argentine Malbec. Yes, we'll take some of that too, please. Thank you."

He hung up and smiled. "What was that for?" she asked.

"I haven't eaten either. It should be here in about thirty minutes."

She shook her head. "I can't let you do that."

Her stomach chose that moment to growl at her. She slapped her hand over it, and Ben laughed. "How can you argue with that?" he said.

"All right, if you insist. But there isn't much space in here." She ran a hand through the mess that was her hair. "Are you sure you don't want me to get dressed, and we can go downstairs?"

He pulled off his suit jacket and shook his head. "I've spent most of the day networking and schmoozing, and I don't want to have to see or talk to anyone else but you tonight."

She quivered at the thought of a whole evening in this hotel room alone with him. "I know what you mean," she said. "It's exhausting, isn't it? I don't do many of these types of events. Usually, it's just me and Sarah in the office all day."

"What about your brother? What does he do for your company?"

"He's my business manager. I do all the programming, and he does everything else. I really couldn't run the company without him." She quickly changed the subject, feeling awkward talking about Daniel with him. "Okay, so if we're staying in, what do you want to do?"

The blush crawled up her neck as soon as the words

were out there. Obvious much? What else did two people who were attracted to each other do when alone in a hotel room with a king-size bed?

He grinned but only said, "You were working before I interrupted you. Why don't I grab some things from my room, and we can work in here, together."

He read her hesitation. "If you're not comfortable with that, I can leave you alone."

"No, it's okay. Dinner is on its way already and I...I do *want* to spend the evening with you. I just don't think this is really what *you* wanted to do with your time, is it?"

He cupped her chin and dragged his thumb over her bottom lip. "Hopefully, we won't work *all* night."

Even as her bones threatened to melt, her knee-jerk reaction was to take him to task for making assumptions, but he wasn't assuming anything, was he? They both knew this thing between them was coming to a head. At least Ben was saying that he would leave it up to her to tell him when she was ready.

She couldn't speak through the lump in her throat and only nodded.

He took her key card with him on the way out. For a long moment, she debated whether or not to jump back into the bathroom and try to bring some order to her hair and put on a little makeup, but stubbornly decided that if he was serious about wanting to work, this was the view he was going to have to deal with.

He returned fifteen minutes later dressed in a pair of cargo shorts and a white T-shirt stretched across his wide chest. She doubted he had intended to throw her senses into a dizzying spiral just by putting on a T-shirt, but that's how she felt. She bit her lip. You'd think she would be immune after their day in the water, but good lord he was a sight to behold.

She had papers spread out across the desk, so she went back to the bed and sat up against the headboard, staring at him while her computer booted up. The only other potential workspace was the coffee table in front of the armchair by the window, so that's where Ben headed.

"Are you sure you're going to be okay like that?" she asked. He'd have to hunch over with his elbows on his knees in order to use the keyboard. "I can move everything off the desk and—"

"Don't worry about me." He smiled. "I'm used to working wherever I can find some peace and quiet. I've even been known to take stuff into the emergency stairwell of my own office building when Nolan's there because there's no getting any peace and quiet with him around. God forbid there's ever a fire and the alarm goes off."

They both laughed. "Sometimes I have to call in 'sick' to my own company, because I'll get more work done if I stay at home with the cell phone stuffed away somewhere so I can't get to it before the voicemail kicks in. It makes me wonder why I bothered to rent office space."

She paused. They'd just shared something about work, and this time it hadn't made her feel like she couldn't breathe, like she was on a one-way train to repeating all of her parents' mistakes. In fact, it had been kind of...nice. The moment dragged out as they grinned at each other until Liz finally dropped her gaze

"Are you planning to stay in the same offices once you roll out nationwide distribution of your program?" he asked.

She shrugged. "It will depend on whether or not Diego Vargas is interested enough to make me an offer."

Damn it. She'd said too much, especially considering that Ben was no doubt planning to meet with Vargas this week also…or maybe he had already. "I didn't mean—" she stammered.

And *now* it was uncomfortable.

He shook his head, and his smile seemed genuine. "I'm sure he'll pull through for you. He'd be crazy not to see the potential in your work."

How would he know? Just how deeply had he investigated Sharkston?

No, it was a harmless comment. No need for her to get squirrelly about it. At least, that's what she was telling herself. Pulling her bottom lip between her teeth, she forced her attention to the computer screen.

Dinner arrived a few minutes later, and her mouth started to water when the server lifted the silver dish covers. She hadn't realized just how hungry she was. Ben cleared off the small table while Liz poured the wine, and they both sat on the floor so they wouldn't have to hunch over to eat.

"Oh God," she moaned around a mouthful of crab cake. "These are to die for."

She shook her head at the plate in front of Ben, almost empty already. "Some things never change. You still attack a meal like it's a race to be won."

He glanced down and grinned. "You mean it isn't?"

She laughed. He reached over and brushed crumbs from her chin. The tiny touch gave her goose bumps.

They talked about everything but business, or about the past, and by the time dinner was done, Liz was surprisingly relaxed. She lifted the cloth napkin to her lips and regretfully looked back at her computer. "I guess I'd better get back to work."

He refilled her wineglass as she got to her feet. "To keep you going," he said with a smile.

He started flipping through a small stack of paperwork. She wasn't surprised that he could so easily shift focus. She might be a decent enough diversion for a little while, but he obviously wasn't tortured with temptation by her very presence, at least not enough to be distracted from what was really important, his work.

She stifled a grimace. She had absolutely no reason to be bitter about that. In fact, she should stop being distracted by *him* and get to work too.

Ben reached into his bag and rummaged for something. When he donned a pair of wire-rimmed glasses, she almost groaned. *Whoa.* And those were new. The glasses added a whole other level of compelling to this man. It left her mouth dry and sent her mind racing with hot nerd fantasies she never even knew she had until this very moment.

What was she saying about focus, again?

His mouth was moving. He had a Bluetooth in his ear and was speaking so quietly she hadn't even realized he was on the phone. Allowing herself one last glance his way, she finally stopped obsessing and turned around, although it took a long time before her determination to focus became a reality.

• • •

Ben was looking over his coding notes one last time when

across the room Beth suddenly jumped up from her seat with a little whoop of excitement.

He looked up over the rim of his glasses and watched her victory dance. Her happiness was infectious, and tension he hadn't even noticed he'd been carrying in his shoulders released.

He glanced down at his watch. It was almost midnight. The few hours since they'd finished dinner passed mostly in easy silence as they worked. Not side-by-side exactly, but close enough that the light scent of her perfume and her occasional mutter of frustration had been a constant and tempting reminder of her presence.

She waved her hands in the air now, swinging her hips back and forth. Her eyes were bright, and she looked relieved. He didn't know what problem she'd just solved, but he certainly liked the end result. Beth deserved this chance to show the world what she could do.

"I did it! I fixed it!" She turned to him with a huge grin on her face. He tossed his glasses to the table and leaned back with crossed arms, admiring the way her body moved. He couldn't tear his gaze away. It didn't matter that she wore only a pair of printed men's boxer shorts and a plain tank top. To him, it was as good—maybe better—than an evening gown. Beth Carlson was a knock-out by any measure.

As she turned to him, her movements slowed. Awareness bloomed in her cheeks, and the knowledge of the effect she had on him lit those devastating green eyes. "Are you still working?" she asked, her voice low and husky.

He shook his head. Which was true, but he could have been right in the middle of the most important task of his job, and he still would have blown it off. For her.

She grinned and leaned over to take his hand and pull him up from the chair. "Then let's celebrate. I don't know about you, but after the day we've had, I think it's definitely time to unwind."

Ben didn't want to make assumptions about what she may or may not be ready for. "Do you want to go out?"

He'd love to get her out on a darkened dance floor. Had been thinking about it since the boat. He wouldn't care what she was wearing as long as it was skimpy as hell, and she moved all up against him, her skin hot and slick, her breathing heavy, her hips driving him crazy.

He tucked his finger under her chin until she lifted her gaze back to his. The chemistry between them was close to exploding. The proof of it was in the sizzle he felt every time he touched her. It was in the widening of her eyes as he looked down into her face.

Yes, they should leave this room. If they went somewhere public, at least he'd have a fighting chance of keeping his hands to himself. And he needed to keep his hands to himself, because he was determined that *she* would be the one to decide when it was time for them to take this thing to the next level. He didn't want her to feel any pressure from him.

But she shook her head. "I don't want to go anywhere," she whispered.

Her hair was loose. She'd been playing with it all night, twisting it around her fingertips and pulling the ends to her mouth to nibble on while she worked. He plunged both his hands into the depths of its softness, cradling her skull and tilting her head up.

Before he kissed her, he needed her to say it. "Then tell

me what you want," he murmured.

"I want to stay here. In this room. With you." She leaned her body against him. "*Not* working."

"Thank God." He crushed her mouth in a hard kiss. A deep kiss. A kiss that immediately sent him reeling, it felt too desperate, too needy.

Afraid of overwhelming her — and maybe himself — he tried to pull it back and go slow, but her fevered response was instant, like a tidal wave crashing in on the shore. They even weaved on their feet as if the force would carry them away beneath the surface.

Her mouth opened under his, and at the first taste of Caribbean spices from dinner and the tangy bite of red wine on her tongue, his need ramped up. He slid his hands under the hem of her thin tank top and pushed it up her torso until it bunched under her breasts. He rubbed thumbs along the hard silk-covered wire sewed into her bra until they met at her sternum and his hands were practically cupping her.

"Lift your arms."

She raised them straight up over her head. "Oh God, yes," she murmured. "Get me out of these clothes fast."

He pulled her shirt off and threw it onto the chair. With his gaze fastened to the sight of her pushing out of a tiny blue silk bra with white lace trim that couldn't possibly have been designed for actual support, he dragged his own shirt over his head and let it fall to the carpet before covering her mouth once again.

She was so hot and sweet and perfect, he could spend forever just kissing her, but soon she broke apart with a sexy pant and lowered her hands to his cargo shorts. She never took her eyes off him, pushing down his shorts, and then hers.

Left in nothing but the pretty bra and a delicate matching thong, she looked like a goddess.

He dragged her against him, pressing a hand to the small of her back as he hooked his other hand under her knee and lifted her leg up his flank. She stood against him, up on her toes, holding on for balance, and he reveled in the sharp sting of her nails digging into his biceps.

"I've been waiting to get you this close again all night," he said.

"You're a master of torture," she whispered. "I probably would have been finished working much earlier if not for the distraction you made just being here in the same room with me."

"I couldn't tell. Maybe because I was busy imagining icy cold showers."

She laughed, all throaty with desire. "Maybe once I get you out of my system, I'll be able to focus better."

"Well, I'm all for giving it a shot." He chuckled, but he didn't like the uncomfortable stab of irritation. The reminder that she was still thinking of the two of them as a simple fling, something for her to use to scratch an itch, bothered him more than he wanted to admit.

She tipped her head all the way back, exposing her throat and lifting her breasts against his chest. He kissed her and wrapped his arms around her, lifting her right off her feet. She wrapped her legs around his waist.

"On the bed or against the wall?"

Chapter Twelve

Liz jerked her head up. "*Wh-what?*"

His smile was playful. "Too late, the decision is mine," he said.

With one knee on the mattress, Ben laid her on the bed and followed her down. She thought she was prepared for the intimacy of this, of him, but was still shocked at the feel of his weight on top of her, solid and heavy like he was going to leave an impression.

He tugged one bra strap off her shoulder and down her arm, then the other. Impatient, she awkwardly twisted her hands behind her back to undo the clasp. He smiled and held her still, gently trapping her arms beneath her.

She gave a little tug, but wasn't going to be able to move unless he shifted position. "What are you doing?"

He lifted a brow, and she realized what a stupid question that was. "I'm doing what I've wanted to do for days."

"Hold me down and take advantage of me?" In fact, that

sounded like a brilliant idea. A deliciously erotic idea. She would be completely on board with such a thing if it meant he was going to do it *now*.

"I'm going to strip these skimpy pieces of silk off you with my own two hands. Maybe with my teeth, and then slowly take my time exploring every inch of your body."

She shuddered, the rush of desire his words evoked sending her into a smoking tailspin. It wasn't until he groaned her name that she realized she was making tight circles against him with her hips, and she'd hooked one ankle over his waist.

"Damn, woman. You're not going to make it easy to go slow, are you?"

"*Slow?*" This was going to be pure torture. Torture designed to make her scream and beg.

He ducked his head and opened his mouth over the silk of her bra while he guided her arms back out from under her. When he lifted his head, she glanced down at the wet circle clinging to her hard nipple. Her chest rose and fell rapidly.

He pulled at the cups of her bra, leaving the band fastened around her so that she could feel the thin shoulder straps teasing her sides.

Then she felt nothing but his tongue and his hands.

He stayed true to his word to take his time. Squirming beneath him, she silently begged him to take her to the next level, but actual coherent words were beyond her ability to manage. And when he finally reached under her to undo the clasp of her bra and flung the garment aside, his mouth trailed a slow, hot, wet path between her breasts all the way to her bellybutton…and then lower.

She buried her hands in his hair as his scratchy chin

scraped the insides of her thighs and his mouth pressed against her.

He built the pressure up and up until she couldn't stand anymore, but he was in complete control, playing her body like a violin and pushing her right over the edge of reason. A startled shout escaped as her core squeezed and convulsed, but he didn't let up until her shuddering subsided and her moans softened to weak whispers.

Her eyelids fluttered open to the magnificent sight of his wide, bronzed body poised above her.

"Let me grab a condom." His voice was husky. His eyes glowed. His jaw clenched. She was mesmerized by the evidence of his arousal. The knowledge that she affected him so strongly made her feel ultra-sexy, maybe even the most powerful woman in the world.

"Box. Bedside table," she said.

He tore open a wrapper, and when he came back over her, he took her mouth in a surprisingly soft kiss. She'd been expecting heat and urgency, but this was tempered by a surprising gentleness as he cupped her face in his hands and pressed his body into hers.

Her heels dug hard into the mattress as she strained to feel everything. She wanted to memorize the experience. Every tingle, every movement, every ache from muscles that hadn't been active like this for far too long.

She gasped at the slow, deliberate intrusion, her fingernails digging crescent moons into Ben's arms. When he was as deep inside her as could be, he stopped kissing her and leaned back. She hadn't even realized she'd clenched her eyes shut until she forced them back open to look up at him.

"What is it?" she squeaked, wondering why he watched

her that way, as if he was looking *into* her, into the private part of her soul where she hid all the insecurities and worries that had formed a part of her, as well as all the dreams and goals she'd been fighting to achieve. "What do you see?"

"Just you." There was something more in his expression than she could decipher. The thumb that traced her lips and smoothed up across the apple of her cheek was tender.

It could just be nostalgia, but what if it wasn't? What if it was something deeper?

She didn't know if she could handle that. Could she take such a risk? Risk meant she had more to lose, and losing Ben again after all this would tear her apart.

"You're so damn beautiful," he said. He planted his arms in the pillow on either side of her head and eased out slowly until she grabbed his hips to keep him with her and he stilled. "Every bit as devastating as I knew you would be, and more so."

She ducked her forehead against his chest, heat flooding her cheeks. Of all the…after everything they'd already gotten up to this week — including being caught topless in the middle of the Caribbean — this is what caused her to blush?

"Beautiful? I guess every woman looks beautiful when she's naked in bed and begging you for more." She forced out a laugh.

"Don't do that." His jaw tightened. "This isn't about 'every woman.' It's about you. Just you and me here together."

Her emotions spiraled out of control. "Oh, Ben."

"Don't get me wrong, I thought you were gorgeous the very first day we met," he continued, lips curling as he tipped her face back up to his. "But now you've got this…glow."

"*Glow?*" Her head thrashed from side to side. "Are

you certain it's not just, ah…" She groaned as she tried to concentrate on his words, but it was so hard when he started to move, stroking her so good. In and out. Long. Deep. *Ahhh Jeez.* "Sure it's not…you know?"

"The lovely flush of sex?" Was he actually teasing her now? He seemed to be having way too much fun with this conversation, while she could barely breathe for wanting him.

She pulled on his arms and hooked her ankles together at the small of his back, teetering on the edge of ecstasy.

"Whatever it is and wherever it comes from, it's beautiful and hot and sexy. And I intend to bask in it." He cupped her breast and lowered his head. "All. Night. Long." Each of his words was punctuated by a killer flick of his tongue against her nipple.

She arched up against him, tightening her thighs around his hips. "Ben, please. I can't take any more. I need…"

"What?" His movements hastened, a deep throaty groan rumbling over her hot and sweaty skin as his mouth traced back up to hers. "What do you need?"

His eyes were dark pools, and she couldn't believe she'd thought he wasn't as affected as she was just because he had been able to retain the gift of speech.

Desire. Need. It was there in his eyes and the hard lines of his face. It was in the tense muscles holding him above her.

"You," she whispered. "I want you."

He dropped his head and rasped her name, making her tremble uncontrollably. She let the rhythm take her over and gave into the tension spiraling within her until it exploded in a massive umbrella of sparks and colors. As she cried out,

Ben did as well. His body shuddered and stiffened above her.

Finally, he pressed his forehead to hers while they both waited for their breathing to calm down. His eyes were closed, and his nose almost touched hers in an Eskimo kiss.

They stayed like that for a long time. When Liz finally shifted one leg off his hip because of a twitching muscle, he pressed a hard kiss on her lips and lifted himself off her.

"Stay right there," he said gently. "Let me dispose of this, and I'll pour what's left of that bottle of wine on my way back."

Right. She glanced down with a nod. The condom. "I still want to try it against the wall," she murmured with a smile.

He chuckled. "Well then in that case, give me a minute and join me in the shower. There's a wall in there we can practice on."

When the door to the bathroom closed, she threw her arm over her head and looked up at the ceiling. Self-consciousness and cold uncertainty started to settle in pretty much immediately.

What was this? Ben had never promised her anything. Certainly not more than the island fling she'd practically asked for that day out on the boat. But he *had* asked her to come to New York with him once. Could those feelings be revived? Could they have something more than just... whatever this was?

Part of her wanted it so badly she could taste it, but she didn't dare let herself think about the logistics of a relationship with someone who not only lived across the country but who also represented her biggest professional competitor...and every deep-seated fear she'd ever had.

She shifted and leaned over the edge of the bed. Her

thong was crumpled up on the floor and she reached down to grab it, then scootched across to the other side of the mattress, looking for her bra, but it wasn't there. Glancing around the room, she finally spotted it on the table where Ben had been working earlier. How the hell had it gotten there?

As she stretched out to grab it, her hand brushed the track pad of his laptop, bringing the screen to bright wakefulness. She politely looked away but the name on the screen had already caught her eye and despite herself, she turned back.

She felt guilty even as she squinted to see more clearly. She was looking at Ben's email inbox, and the message at the top of the list was from Jemarcho's president, with a re: line that read "Investment Offer."

Crap. Crap. Crap. The convention just got started! She wanted to believe that there was some other reason why Diego Vargas would email Ben about an investment offer already, other than the one that alternatively meant she would *not* be getting such an email, either now or after her company received Tyson Wallace's stamp of approval.

And he'd known. This email had already been read. But when? Before or after he'd told her he was "sure" Vargas would invest in Sharkston?

The time stamp on the message was from early that evening. She noticed then that the message directly below it was from Ben's partner, Steve Nolan. The subject line on that one was "Distraction plan working—keep it up." Her stomach bottomed out as she realized what that must mean. All her fledgling hopes for a future with Ben washed away like cloudy water down the drain.

The water in the bathroom turned off. Liz slapped the

screen of Ben's laptop down and jerked back to the middle of the bed, clutching the sheet to her bare chest.

He came into the room with a devastating, expectant smile that was like a knife in her heart, but his expression changed almost immediately when he looked at her.

His gaze shifted to the table and back. His lips pressed into a thin line. Yeah, he knew what she'd seen. "You couldn't help yourself?" he said flatly. "I suppose it's my fault for not turning off the computer."

She was *not* going to defend herself. "And I suppose you just couldn't help playing games?"

"What games? What do you think it is that you saw?"

"Enough to know you're getting exactly what you wanted all over the damn place, and I'm going to be left out in the cold."

"So you spy on someone else's emails, jump to a few conclusions, and that's it? You think you know everything? You don't even want to talk about it?"

"What's there to talk about? How do you plan to explain yourself?"

"I've done nothing that I need to explain to you, but I'm more than willing to talk things out reasonably."

"Why, so you can *distract* me some more?" Her voice wavered as the words of his partner's email swam before her vision. Maybe she was wrong about what she'd seen. Maybe there *was* some explanation. She would never have believed that Ben could... She clenched her jaw tight. She hated herself for the way she was acting, but couldn't seem to help it. This wasn't college anymore, but Ben was *still* beating her at *everything*. Only now he was also beating her heart to a bloody pulp, too. She needed time to think. "You should probably go."

"Well, I wanted to get you out of my system once and for all. I guess this makes it easy." He bent to grab his shorts and shirt and pulled them on with quick, sharp movements while she watched as if through a haze, swallowing past the bitter tasting lump in her throat.

Finally, he picked up his laptop and his bag and walked to the door, just like that.

Liz smashed her fist into the bedcovers gathered in her lap. She opened her mouth to speak. The words wouldn't come. Watching him walk out wasn't what she really wanted, but she couldn't do it, couldn't tell him to stay. Those words on the screen kept flashing in front of her eyes. *Keep it up.*

He stopped at the door and turned around. Obvious regret shone from his eyes as he shrugged the strap of his bag over his shoulder.

Then he was gone.

She curled up in a ball, wrapping her arms around her knees as she stared at the door. Tears tracked down her face and fell off her chin. She swiped the back of her hand over her eyes and buried her face in the pillow…just in case he could hear through the walls.

Chapter Thirteen

For the first time she could remember, Liz awoke before her alarm. But really, she'd been up most of the night, the look on Ben's face haunting her. He had been…hurt.

She spent an hour sitting up in bed in the early morning shadows, staring at the digital lines on the bedside clock and reliving the way she'd reacted last night. Of course he was right. She'd jumped to conclusions, which, even if they were true, was no reason for her to have acted like a brat having a hissy fit. And she shouldn't have sent him away without at least talking things through.

But she'd been hurt too, damn it.

Would she have felt so irrational if they hadn't just had the most intense sex of her life? If he hadn't baldly admitted that he'd slept with her to "get her out of his system"? He'd never handled failure well—maybe because he rarely failed at anything—but she hadn't expected him to consider her refusal to go to New York as one. Suddenly, it all felt like a game, a game she should have known he was playing. Turning her into an idiot, a dupe.

Ben Harrison scrambled her brains, put holes in her good sense, and churned up all her emotions. Had she really thought she could handle him on a personal level and still do her job here this week? *Ha!*

Finally, she got up and took a shower, then, with a renewed determination that the game wasn't over yet, she went to talk to Daniel. She knocked on his door a couple of times and was relieved when he opened it.

"Hi," she said. "Do you have a few minutes?"

"Sure." He waved her inside. Overall, he looked better than he had yesterday.

"We need to fine-tune our strategy if we're going to get those investment dollars," she said after he closed the door behind her. "Optimus Inc. has been wining and dining Diego Vargas, and I think they're close to swaying him over to their side, so we have to up our game."

Daniel crossed his arms. "Does that mean you're done being Harrison's best girl?"

She squared her shoulders and narrowed her gaze. "It means that we've *both* been vacationing long enough. Let's get down to business."

He nodded. "You're right, but I've been talking to Vargas, too."

"You have? When?"

"We ran into each other last night. He said he'd received the portfolio we sent him and was very impressed with the material and the calculations we'd made."

"I emailed that package late last night. He had to have looked at it almost immediately. When did you talk to him?"

Maybe that meant Vargas hadn't already made his decision. That the email Ben received hadn't been a solid offer, and Sharkston still had a shot. "Where did you meet him?"

"Just out and about the resort. It was pretty late."

Her chest constricted, but she couldn't do it. She couldn't ask. If she mentioned the poker game, he would think she didn't trust him. Maybe worse, if she mentioned the poker game, and he hadn't gotten wind of it from someone else already, she might be the one who ended up knocking him off the wagon.

"Well, did he say anything else?" she asked.

"I think he's looking to make a bigger commitment. What if he offered to buy our program outright? It would sway him over to our side for sure, and we'd be talking about a lot more money."

"What? Why would we agree to something like that? After all the work we've done, we don't want to just give it all up. Diego Vargas will get his money's worth out of any investment he makes, but he's not going to buy us out. That's not what we're looking for." She was shocked Daniel would even suggest it. "Right? I thought we were both on the same page about that."

"It was just a suggestion," he said quickly. "So then what do you think we should do?"

They hashed out a plan for selling Vargas on investing in Sharkston instead of Optimus, and then Liz left Daniel to get dressed.

On the way to the convention rooms, she stopped for coffee. There was a long lineup, and Liz craned her neck to look over the heads of the customers ahead of her to see if Ben was there. She told herself it was a good thing he wasn't, because as much as they needed to talk, she would take as much of a reprieve from that discussion as she could get.

She glanced out the big windows. Clouds blanketed the horizon again today.

"They're sayin' the big storm might blow over," said a voice behind her.

She turned and smiled at the portly gentleman in line behind her. Wire-rimmed spectacles perched on top of his head, almost buried in his thick mop of silver hair. He wore a pair of boldly patterned Bermuda swimming trunks and a neon yellow tank top with the kind of leather sandals that strapped across the foot with two lengths of Velcro. There was a beach towel over his shoulder, and he carried a copy of the *New York Times* tucked into his armpit.

"That would be wonderful, wouldn't it?"

"Ayup, but who really knows? None of them weather experts ever seem to get it right."

She chuckled and looked back out the window. There was just a slight sway to the tall palm trees lining the walking paths of the resort grounds, but nothing to suggest a big storm was about to hit.

She nodded to the beach towel. "Are you off to get some time in at the pool in case the storm does come later?"

"Ayup. This is my first vacation in thirty years. The missus and I planned it for a long time before we were able to get the money together." He frowned and swallowed hard. "Never thought I'd end up going without her, but I suppose I ought to make the most of it."

She felt a pang of sadness and put her hand on his arm before she even realized she was doing it. "I'm sure she's here with you in spirit."

"Thank you." He patted her fingers until she pulled back. "You with that fancy group, what's all about the computer stuff?"

"Yes. It's a nice excuse to go on a trip like this," she said with an upbeat smile. The line started to move forward again, and she was next at the counter.

As she took her coffee and waved good-bye she said, "Nice to meet you. Have a good day."

The conversation she'd just had would never have occurred back home. Everyone was always in such a hurry to lock themselves away in an office for the day, they'd never have "wasted" time talking to a stranger. Even now, she walked along swiftly as if she were on a strict schedule. When she realized it, she took a deep breath and forced herself to slow down and actually take note of her surroundings.

It was a beautiful resort. The gardens and far-off vistas visible through the windows were breathtaking, and there was no need for her to be anywhere in a hurry. The convention was well underway, but the first seminar of the day was still half an hour from now, and she didn't actually have a hard appointment until her seminar with Ben later. As much as she was dreading that now, it was freeing to have some time to kill, and she found herself smiling back at the people in the halls.

She half expected to run into Ben at every corner, but when she'd gotten all the way to the entrance of the lobby and he hadn't appeared, she tried telling herself it wasn't disappointment she felt.

She didn't know what she would say if she actually stumbled across him right now anyway. She was still hurt, but there was also a hard ball of guilt sitting on her chest.

She'd violated his privacy and then reacted harshly. Maybe he hadn't felt the need to explain himself, but he'd wanted to talk and she hadn't let him.

Turning down a hallway, she ran into Steve Nolan again, thankfully this time without physically bowling him over with her coffee. "Good morning, Ms. Carlson," he said with a bright smile.

As genuine as he seemed, her back went right up, and her temper flared.

He stood there looking down at her, confident and sure of himself just like Ben. "I know you and your partner think you've got everything in the bag, but—"

Suddenly, another suit appeared at his side. Liz knew who it was even before she looked up. She tried to ignore the jump in her pulse.

"Don't take your disappointment out on him," Ben said in a low voice. "He has nothing to do with this."

He could wear all the perfectly cut power suits he wanted and stare at her with those intense crystal blue eyes all day long, and it wouldn't make any difference. "The two of you are in this together, so I assume he's adopted your adage. Whatever it takes to get ahead, didn't you say that just yesterday?" She alternated her glare between Harrison and Nolan. So much for apologizing to him. As soon as he'd stopped in front of her, all she saw was red.

"Beth," he warned.

She poked him in the chest with a hiss. "Are you seriously going to pretend that you haven't been purposely trying to distract me—oh, and getting me 'out of your system,' of course. Can't forget that." She practically snarled and pointed at Nolan angrily. "While *he* wines and dines Diego

Vargas behind my back?"

His expression had turned to stone as he looked down at her.

"Nobody has done anything behind your back."

"Are you so ruthless that you can't stand some *honest* competition?"

His jaw clenched. "Why don't we take this discussion elsewhere?"

She looked around them at the people milling about in small groups and put her hands on her hips. "Why? Are you afraid someone will realize you're nothing but a big corporate shark?"

His hard expression turned into a laugh, and he crossed his arms. "Beth, every one of the people at this convention *already* believes that, because they're the same way. They all recognize the reality of doing business."

"So all that stuff about not wanting to step on people on your way to the top was just bullshit."

He frowned. "That's not what I meant."

Beside them, Nolan cleared his throat. "Why don't I let the two of you continue your discussion without me?"

Both of them nodded but didn't notice when he turned away. Her focus was on Ben. For good or bad, he would always consume the bulk of her attention whenever they were in a room together.

He looked over her shoulder, and his mouth pressed into a thin line. He took her hand and pulled her along with him down the hall.

"I don't want to go anywhere with you," she protested, but she realized that people had indeed started to watch them with avid curiosity. Because of the competition, she and Ben were already the focus of so much attention, and the prospect of a juicy scandal would only set fire to the wagging tongues.

They entered an empty conference room. There were thirty or forty chairs set up theatre style in front of a short podium with a microphone. Ben shut the door, twisted the lock, and put his back to it as he turned to her with a frown.

"I shouldn't have walked out last night without insisting that we talk this through," he said. "But now you're going to listen to me."

"Oh really?" She snorted, arms crossed. "And you're going to keep me locked up in here until I do? What kind of threat is that?"

"Shit, Beth. I'm not threatening you." He closed his eyes and ran a hand through his hair.

For some reason, his frustration broke through her anger. With a sigh, she took a step back. "Fine, let's talk then."

He looked down at her. "The truth is that Nolan *did* suggest I keep you occupied, because he figured it would give him an opportunity to get some extra time with Diego Vargas, but that isn't why I was with you last night. You *know* that." His voice was edged with steel.

"Oh, so it was just convenient," she snapped. "You get laid, *and* your company gets the investment it needs."

"I haven't gotten any commitment from Vargas yet," he admitted, his words clipped and short. "The email he sent me was a request for some numbers which, I might add, he mentioned asking for from your company as well."

"Oh." She had started to think that might be the case but had still been too hurt by the second email from his partner for it to make much of a difference in the heat of the moment.

"Have I done anything in the last few days to keep you from making appointments or talking to people about your work while you're here?"

"No," she said quickly.

"And I certainly didn't sleep with you as part of some disgusting plot to undermine your efforts and push your company out of the running with Vargas."

"I know. You were right," she interrupted, feeling more awful with every word. "I was feeling vulnerable last night, and I already realized that I probably jumped to conclusions."

He took her hand and squeezed. "Listen, I realize we're both here for the same thing, and for one of us to be successful it means that the other likely won't be," he said gently. "But that part of it isn't personal. I thought we agreed that what we do for our companies professionally wouldn't affect what happens between us personally."

Had they actually made such a promise? It would have been a good idea, right? A promise like that might have meant she wouldn't have made such a horrible mess of this situation.

"As for getting you out of my system…sure, I hoped I could, especially when you only seemed interested in an island fling and nothing more." He slipped his hand up her arm and curved around the back of her neck, making her knees weak. "But it's not working."

The rare vulnerability in the simple statement, and the fact that he refused to look away, letting her see all the way inside him, frightened her more than she'd even thought possible. She had to be strong. "Can we start over and pretend last night never happened?" she asked, breathless.

"I couldn't forget last night even if I wanted to."

She groaned. "Can we at least agree that it's a bad idea to repeat it?"

If these last few days—and last night in particular—had proved anything, it was that Liz obviously wasn't as different from her parents as she'd always tried to be. She was just as driven, just as determined to succeed. She didn't want to give up on everything she'd worked so hard for, not even to give love a chance. She loved her work, and she wanted to win this competition and get the investment money from Vargas so badly her fists were clenched at her sides.

And that meant the decision she'd made a year ago had been the right one, the only choice she could have made. She'd experienced firsthand how destructive it was for two people like her and Ben to be together. They could never have a serious relationship. How could two wrongs ever make anything right?

He frowned. "Is that really what you want?"

"I think it would be for the best, don't you?" She backed away.

"Not especially." He didn't follow, but stayed where he was against the conference room door with arms crossed, watching her. "Now that we've agreed to keep our business goals separate from everything else, tell me…we had a good time out on the boat, didn't we?"

She nodded. That had been amazing. "Anyone would have had a good time snorkeling in the crystal clear waters of an island paradise for the day."

"But we've also proven that we can work together pretty well, haven't we?"

She shrugged. "To a limited extent, sure."

"And there's no doubt we're fantastic in bed together."

She blushed and nodded. "But that's not—"

"Do you have plans this evening?"

She shook her head.

"Then have dinner with me after we finish our seminar this afternoon."

"Nobody can have it all, Ben," she murmured, her heart in her throat.

"How do you know until you try?"

God, he sounded so sure of himself. If only she could be as certain of anything. She swallowed hard. "I know. Trust me, I wish I didn't, but I know what it's like to be part of something that should have been wondrous and special, but ended up lessened because of ego and selfishness."

"Beth."

"No." She looked away, angry with herself for succumbing to the past yet again. "I never want to feel that way again, to be second to anyone's career."

"It doesn't—"

"And I won't do the same to someone else. I won't turn love into indifference. I won't let something beautiful and bright be warped into regret and resentment."

He sighed. "Then let me show you that at least we can still be friends."

"What will that prove? What does any of it prove?"

"Maybe nothing," he said in a low voice. "But maybe something. Something we both need to figure out once and for all."

She didn't dare agree with that. "How about we just try to get through the rest of the day and see how it goes." She stopped and cocked her head at the sound of muffled voices and knocking coming from the other side of the door.

"Wait," she whispered, pulling at his sleeve and looking over her shoulder at all the empty chairs. "Is someone trying to get in here?" All the meeting rooms in the resort had been booked by the convention organizers for seminars and workshops. *Of course* someone was trying to get in here. "What time is it?"

He checked his watch. "Time for someone's seminar?"

She gasped, but then she pictured a bunch of confused corporate types staring at the closed door and a giggle escaped. More knocking. She slapped her hand over her mouth to stifle her laughter, but couldn't seem to stop.

"They're going to think we're doing…something…in here," she squeaked.

"Something?" He waggled his eyebrows and made her giggle harder, until he reached over and brushed an errant lock of hair behind her ears and she froze, tingles dancing across her skin. "Nobody is going to think anything except that we were using the space to get ready for our presentation later today."

With that he straightened his suit and winked at her before unlocking the door.

A flustered looking woman with a "convener" badge stumbled into the room. She'd paired a brown business jacket with a narrow pencil skirt that went past her knees and kept her from taking full strides, making her look a little like a shuffling twig. Behind her was a crowd of at least twenty people, all of whom started to brush past her like water flowing around a rock in the stream.

"Excuse me," the convener said in a chilly voice. "But you shouldn't be in here. This room is needed for a seminar now."

"Of course. We're finished. I apologize for the inconvenience." Ben turned a smile on the woman that would have melted a glacier.

It took less than a second, and her frown disappeared. "It's no problem, sir. We still have plenty of time to get ready. Are you able to stay for the discussion?"

"Thank you, ma'am, I'd love to," he said.

She flushed and smiled, reaching up to adjust her thick black librarian glasses. "Oh, I'm just Marjorie, sir. Marjorie Lamb."

"Nice to meet you Marjorie. I'm Ben."

Completely impressed, Liz watched as Ben and Marjorie chatted like old friends for a whole minute, talking about the convention and the coming storm. Finally, the woman jumped to attention and rushed to the front of the room to organize the speakers, throwing a wistful look over her shoulder every so often.

Liz found a seat in the front of the room and reached into her bag for her tablet. She had indeed planned on attending this seminar and wanted to take good notes.

Empty handed, Ben fell into the chair beside her and propped an ankle on his knee as the three speakers took their positions. She recognized one as James Kronan, president of Gemini—a company that had been the new kid on the block at this very convention only four years ago, just like Sharkston and Optimus Inc. were this year—and the other two were his top engineers.

"You could give this presentation, you know that, right?" Ben leaned close and whispered into her ear.

"Oh shut up. I'm not even close to being as qualified as

these guys are." She gestured toward the company president waiting patiently at the front of the room for everyone to settle down. "Don't you know who that is?"

"Yes, and I also know that you understood more about these algorithms when you were still in college than he ever—"

"Shh." She squeezed his forearm in warning, because if she slapped her hand over his mouth to shut him up someone might have noticed. "It doesn't matter what he does or doesn't know about algorithms, because he was obviously smart enough to *hire* people who do. The best in the business, in fact." She nodded toward the other two guys, who were coming up the aisle to join him. They all took their seats at the table.

"Not the best," said Ben with a grin, "because they didn't hire you, and they didn't hire me."

"Flattery isn't going to help your case with me. Now cut it out; they're getting started." She turned her head and smiled behind her hand as the convener stepped up to the front and tapped the microphone.

As the seminar got underway, someone sat down on the other side of her. When that space had been empty, she'd been able to ignore just how big and close and solid Ben was on the other side of her, but now that she was bookended in her seat, he seemed to take up more and more of the available space until she found herself taking short breaths to keep from reacting to his nearness.

He didn't touch her in any way, didn't send her sidelong looks or whisper into her ear. To every other person in the room, they were just two business associates sitting side by side.

A little thrill went through her at the idea of having an

exciting secret, a reckless wild side that she could indulge, in the form of Ben Harrison. After her parents died, she'd spent a long time being afraid of losing anyone else. Fear and caution had ruled her life. This week was teaching her—in more ways than one—that sometimes calculated risks were worth taking. As long as she stayed in control, and as long as she didn't risk more than she could afford to lose.

Ben spoke up and asked the panel of speakers a question. Surprisingly, it was the exact same thing she would have asked. Liz nodded in agreement at the answer, but felt there was still a gray area. She started to ask a follow-up question of her own. "Oh wait, I'm sorry," she said to Ben when she realized she'd interrupted. "I didn't mean to—"

He grinned. "No problem, Ms. Carlson. I was going to follow up with the same question myself."

The seminar continued in that vein, due in large part to her and Ben. They hadn't exactly taken over, but she had a feeling from the looks on the convener's face that they'd definitely brought more audience participation to the event than had been expected. In fact, the seminar turned into quite a lively discussion, and Liz and Ben were actually answering as many questions as they were asking.

She hoped the panelists weren't upset, but she didn't think they would be. After all, this was much more memorable than listening to an hour's worth of lecturing on what could have been a very dry subject. It made her realize just how savvy Ben's suggestion had been to encourage free discussion when it was their turn to get up there later that afternoon.

When the hour was up, almost everyone was slow to move along, and there was a long line at the front to thank the panelists for a great experience.

Ben had been pulled into a small group, so Liz made her way to the door when someone called after her. "Ms. Carlson, please wait."

She turned around as one of the panelists, James Kronan, approached. He shook her hand. "I wanted to tell you that I've been following your work."

She blinked. Had she heard him right? "*My* work?"

"Yes. You're the president of Sharkston Co. aren't you?"

"Yes, but—"

"I read about your programming initiatives in the material distributed in the convention packages with some interest. Your ideas are smart and innovative. When are you scheduled to release your product to market?"

Her heart thumped. "Well, that depends on our ability to raise the investment capital we're looking for."

"I understand that Tyson Wallace is considering your company for his annual endorsement. That should help your visibility immensely."

She smiled. "That's what we're hoping, Mr. Kronan."

"Good luck," he said. "Although I have to admit, if I thought you'd take me up on it, I'd be trying to convince you to join my company."

She laughed. "Perhaps we can negotiate a contract arrangement instead."

"I'd be happy to discuss terms at your convenience."

"I'll remember that," she said. "Thank you for your time. It was a pleasure to meet you."

She could barely contain herself as Kronan said goodbye. Had anyone else seen that? She looked around. Someone had to have witnessed the president of Gemini talking to her like an industry equal.

Chapter Fourteen

Ben stood across the room, watching Beth. He didn't know what James Kronan was talking to her about, but whatever it was had put a wide grin on her face.

How many people would kick up a fuss if he went over there right now and kissed her? Beth would. Beth would hate that. And truthfully, as much as he wanted her, he wanted to help keep that look on her face even more.

She had shone during the seminar. Her questions had been enlightened, and as the discussion became freer, her comments had impressed not only him but everyone else as well.

He excused himself from the people still mingling around him and went to her side. "Do you want to take some time now to go over our material?"

The smile stayed in her expressive eyes, making them sparkle like jewels as she looked up at him, but she shook her head. "I think we'll be fine, and I should really find

Daniel, see if he's going to make it to the seminar."

Something in her gaze held him in place for a moment longer, but eventually he nodded and stepped back. "I'll see you later, then. Text me if you need anything."

As Ben left her, Nolan was waiting for him outside the conference room. "We've got a problem," he said with a frown.

"What kind of problem?"

Nolan nodded politely as other conference attendees passed them on their way to lunch. "Have you been talking to that reporter?" he asked.

"What the hell do you think?"

"I think somehow she knows about Jeffrey Olsen, and she's threatening to print the story."

Ben stopped. "What? How?"

Nolan sent him a hard look. "You tell me."

"No. Beth would never use that kind of information against a competitor, any competitor. It isn't in her blood."

"You're sure about that?"

"Let it go," he snapped, not wanting to hear another word. "It doesn't matter, anyway. I'm not proud of the way I treated Olsen, but the police already cleared me of any responsibility for his death."

"You know it's not about the facts."

"If it looks like we're going to lose out on an investment opportunity because of it, I'll back out and leave you—"

"You'll do no such thing." Nolan scowled. "Listen, you needed to know about the story, but maybe it won't make any difference. This is a small industry, and you weren't the only person to dump Olsen because of his bad business practices...you were just the *last* person."

"We'll see." He wasn't so sure about that, but surprisingly, it didn't feel as important as it had once been to manage the threat. He'd already decided to find a better way of doing business even before seeing Beth again, but she had made him realize who he was doing it *for*.

She'd been right about his goals being out of whack. He'd always been driven by the need to prove himself to the father who had rejected him. Ironically, he'd always known that was the one man who would never be impressed, no matter how successful Ben became.

If he was going to be a *real* success, then he had to do it for himself, and the only way he would ever be satisfied is if he could still look himself in the mirror at the end of every day.

"On another note," Nolan said. "I think Sharkston is making Jemarcho an offer."

"You mean Jemarcho is making *them* an offer?"

"No, I mean exactly what I said. I don't think Ms. Carlson is looking for an investment for her programming platform anymore. She's looking to *sell* it."

Ben frowned. "That doesn't make any sense. Why would Beth want to sell now that she's so close to getting it off the ground on her own?"

"Whether it makes sense or not, it's true. I overheard her partner discussing it with Vargas over a table this morning while you and Carlson were in that morning session. And Vargas looked more than interested. You know he'll jump on it. If he has the chance to buy the rights to that program of theirs, he'll make a lot more money than if he simply took a percentage deal with either one of our companies, even at a generous interest rate."

If Beth had truly decided to pull a fast one, he and Nolan wouldn't be able to talk Diego Vargas into investing. If Optimus Inc. managed to get Tyson Wallace's endorsement, they could find the money they needed somewhere else, but then they'd also be directly competing; not with a company like Sharkston whose profile and resources matched their own, but with Jemarcho Inc., a global powerhouse that had distribution connections all over the world. It would be a slaughter.

Ben ran a hand through his hair and sighed. "Okay, let me handle it. I'll see if I can talk to Vargas after the seminar this afternoon. He might still decide that what we can offer is better suited to his needs, and I might be able to convince him that he doesn't want the expense and hassle of having to run and maintain the programming in-house. He doesn't have the expertise and manpower for that—"

"He will if he hires Sharkston's president on as part of the deal."

"Is that what he said?"

Nolan shrugged. "It's what I would do if I wanted to make sure the product I just bought launched successfully."

Would Beth really be looking to sell and become just another employee of Diego Vargas's company after all the work she'd done? If he didn't know her so well, he would say no, but unfortunately he could see how that might appeal to her. She'd chosen to remain in Seattle because it was familiar and safe, denying the two of them a chance at a real relationship out of fear that the past would repeat itself.

He understood, but he was disappointed, too.

But after the last few days, he'd begun to think she'd conquered her fears. Starting her own business and trying to launch a brand new program had been a risk. Coming to Antigua looking for investment capital had been another risk. He'd started to hope that she was finally ready to take a risk on something more personal too, enough that he'd begun to think this could be about something more than just scratching an itch and walking away. Enough that he'd even considered opening himself up to the possibility of her rejection a second time around.

Idiot. The way she'd reacted last night—as if she'd been *looking* for a reason to mistrust him—and now this... Beth would always find a reason not to risk her future.

Or maybe it was just that she'd never be ready to risk it on *him*.

Either way, he could see failure staring him right in the eyes, a position he'd sworn he would never willingly put himself in again, not with her and not with anyone else. It left a bitter taste in his mouth.

He went to lunch with Nolan and then to his room to get some notes for the seminar. When he met up with Beth back in the conference room, her brother wasn't with her, but she looked refreshed and energized. He could almost believe she was ready to take on the world.

"Is there anything we should go over quickly before we get started?" she asked with a smile.

"No, let's just get this over with."

She looked surprised by his short response, but he couldn't bring himself to play these games with her anymore. Especially now that he knew she'd already given up, that she would never be brave enough to take a real chance...on him or anything else.

They took their places at the front and watched as the

room filled up with attendees. He was a little surprised at the number of faces in the audience. A few bodies even leaned up against the back wall when all the seats had been filled. The convention had been promoting their little competition, their pictures and bios had even gone up on the website the morning after he and Beth had agreed to do it. But Ben still hadn't really expected so many people to take such an interest.

They'd already decided that he would be the one to begin, with a short introduction about himself and his company. He kept it light and brief, and then turned to Beth. She did the same, introducing herself and Sharkston Co. and then smoothly transitioning into the ethics discussion they had prepared. She mesmerized everyone with her smooth voice and confident delivery. Her smile was genuine, and she made eye contact with the audience as she spoke.

They played off one another perfectly, alternating being the one talking at just the right moments, and overall, engaging the audience in a lively discussion worth remembering. By the end of it, Ben was starting to think Nolan must have been wrong in what he'd heard earlier. The woman standing up here with him was passionate about her work and couldn't possibly have given up on her dreams so quickly and easily.

As interesting as he was certain they'd been, theirs was the last seminar of the afternoon and dinner on a Caribbean island awaited. Most of the room cleared pretty quickly.

He looked over the shoulders of the few people sticking around to continue to make points they'd held onto during the formal discussion. One guy in particular hung back to talk to Beth. He wore business casual khakis and a plaid button-down shirt, and seemed pretty animated. She looked a little uncomfortable with the adoring attention and flinched as he alternated between pushing his glasses back up the bridge of his nose and waving his arms as he spoke.

Ben watched out of the corner of his eye. The guy had taken her hand now. She tried tugging it back from his pudgy grip. During the session he was the one who'd been asking all the really specialized questions. After Beth answered the first one with an insight and knowledge even Ben himself could not have matched, the techie had looked at her as if it was love at first sight. Beth wasn't as adept at managing pushy people as he had learned to be.

He couldn't hear what the guy was saying to her now, but from the shuttered look of dismay on Beth's face as she anxiously glanced anywhere but at him and hid her hand behind her back when he tried to grab it again, it may have been a dinner invitation…

She finally jerked her head around and lifted wide eyes to Ben for help.

Worse than dinner. She must be receiving an impromptu marriage proposal.

He chuckled and shook his head. *Congratulations*, he mouthed.

She glared back at him. *Jerk*.

Finally the man pumped her hand vigorously—twice—and turned to leave. Ben met Beth at the door, and they walked to the hotel lobby together, losing the last few hangers-on to the bar, from which raucous conversation and laughter emanated. He found himself glancing down at her over and over again.

As they neared the elevators she stopped. "Is your invitation to dinner tonight still open?"

He hesitated but when her expression fell, he said, "Of course. Why do you have to ask?"

She laughed a little hesitantly. "For some reason, I thought you might have changed your mind."

He didn't *know* his own mind anymore. "And you? How many times did you change your mind?"

"Only about a thousand," she whispered, tilting her head with her gaze fixed on his mouth.

"No more. We see this through," he said to himself as much as to her.

She nodded.

"Good. Meet me here in an hour."

. . .

"Daniel, where have you been?" On a hunch, Liz had walked into the bar before going upstairs to get ready for dinner, and found him there nursing a drink. "I haven't been able to get in touch with you all day, and you missed the seminar."

"I'm sorry," he said, "but I didn't think you needed me there. I knew you would do great, you always do. So I spent some time talking to Vargas, and I need to talk to you about—"

"Ms. Carlson, it's lovely to see you again."

Laura Denham had approached. For the first time Liz noticed there were *two* glasses on the bar in front of Daniel. She returned the woman's warm, friendly smile and shook her hand. "Laura, it's nice to see you too. But please call me Liz."

Laura took her seat next to Daniel, and her smile turned soft and shy. Suddenly Liz felt very much like an intruder. "Well, I had better go get ready for dinner," she said, eager to leave the couple alone. "Daniel, why don't we talk more first thing in the morning?"

He opened his mouth as if to object, but then he nodded instead. "Sure thing, sis."

Laura clapped her hands. "Oh, are you going to the dinner show tonight? The resort has scheduled a special presentation just for the convention, and I hear it's fantastic." She glanced toward Daniel expectantly, and Daniel smiled shyly back at her. Liz had a feeling that's exactly what the two of them would be doing tonight.

She said good night and headed to her room, smiling to herself all the way up the empty elevator. She had no idea where Laura Denham called home in her everyday life. Maybe she lived all the way across the country, and she and Daniel were destined to have only a short-lived affair, but it was still nice to see her brother smile. He deserved to have a little bit of fun.

And that's exactly what she wanted to do tonight now that her work was done. The vote and the closing luncheon speech was tomorrow, but she and Ben had agreed to divide it up between them and she had a good idea what she was going to say.

If Daniel had indeed made progress with Diego Vargas, she could talk to her brother tomorrow, and now that she'd seen him with Laura Denham, she wouldn't have to worry that he'd be sitting at a poker table all night.

The seminar had gone even better than she'd hoped. Ben, of course, had been right, and the two of them proved to be a great team. Today had even made her wonder what might have happened if she'd been brave enough to go to New York with him.

For the first time since sending him away, she regretted the decision. She'd never even given them a chance! What if they could have compromised on the personal and professional fronts and found the kind of work/life balance her parents never had? They might have found something special, become an unstoppable force of nature, but now she would never know.

The sun was setting behind a covering of heavy clouds that gave weight to the early evening shadows, but as Liz opened the French doors to her balcony and walked out, the grounds of the resort buzzed with life and possibility. She turned her face into the breeze. It smelled of salt and sand and the coming rainstorm. She leaned over the white wrought iron railing, breathing it in and feeling strangely free, and yet a little maudlin at the same time.

When she went back inside, she took extra time getting ready for dinner. Looking into the bathroom mirror, she felt like the opposite of the business professional who'd spoken about algorithms, latent variable modelling, and ethics coding all day. The woman looking back at her was someone who went snorkeling with sharks, stood up in front of a room full of industry leaders to teach *them* something, and dared to have a fiery affair with the most devastatingly handsome man she'd ever known.

All of these accomplishments would have been virtually unthinkable to her a few days ago, but if this time with Ben had taught her anything, it was that her fears had cheated her out of too many experiences already, and she didn't want to lose any more.

That comment about "getting her out of his system," thrown out in anger, meant she was taking a bigger risk of being hurt than she would have liked. But sometimes taking risks was necessary, both personally and professionally. If you didn't risk anything, you would never have anything worth losing.

She patted her carefully tamed hair and lined her eyelids with thick dark pencil. She even curled her lashes. She leaned back from the mirror and gasped. Her green eyes looked impossibly wide. Her glossy red lips matched her short, red dress. She'd thrown the outfit in her suitcase not because it was sexy, but because it was light-weight and she didn't have a lot of clothes that would qualify as island-worthy. But maybe she'd gone too far. This didn't even feel like her.

Hell, that was probably a good thing. When she was with Ben, she felt as if there was a better person on the verge of coming out. Someone braver, more daring. Someone smarter and stronger. He made her want to take the risks she'd always shied away from, and made her think that trusting someone with more than just her body or her friendship, but also her past and her future, might not be such a far off possibility as it had once seemed.

She took a deep breath and turned away from the mirror.

He was waiting in the lobby when she got downstairs. She watched him for a few seconds before he noticed her. He looked fantastic as always, one hand under his jacket in his pants pocket. But that wasn't what got her heart racing. It was the approachable smile that stretched across his face as a stranger walked by and said hello, and the way he held himself with cool confidence even though she knew that he doubted some of the decisions he'd made.

Everything about him screamed success. There was no doubt that he was well on his way to achieving everything he'd ever wanted. She only wanted him to remember what he'd told her earlier, that the adventure and challenge of it was all part of the journey. In fact, she wanted to be the one who made sure the spark in his eyes wouldn't ever go out again.

Her heart thudded. It didn't matter what she wanted, did it? Ben may have talked about second chances while he was in her bed during the heat of the moment, but that was then.

Snooping in his email had changed everything.

That investment money from Vargas—whoever it went to—would change everything.

After tomorrow their time was effectively up. She would be going back to Seattle, and he would return to New York.

Maybe it was enough that they'd had these few days… that they would have tonight.

He spotted her.

Immediately, he took several strides across the lobby until he was right in front of her. His expression had changed that quickly from light and friendly to hot, intense, and focused.

"You look ready to set the world on fire," he murmured into her ear. He set *her* on fire, especially as his sizzling gaze traveled the length of her body. "Shall we go to dinner, or just skip the civilized part of the evening altogether?"

She was so tempted, but then he laughed. "You know what? We'd better eat. We're going to need the calories later."

She took his arm, curving her fingers over the hard muscles hidden beneath his jacket. They made their way outside and she looked up into the sky, but was disappointed when there were no stars. They followed the path and the strains of vibrant folk music down to the beach. The way was lit with torches, and when they got to the open tent that had been set up near the water's edge Liz stopped and looked around, amazed. "This is gorgeous."

More torches circled the perimeter of the tent. As she and Ben stepped inside, lanterns from the canvas ceiling cast beautiful shadows on the colorfully dressed tables that had been set up on a wooden platform over the sand and topped with candles. A stage had also been set up at the front end of the tent, and a group of men dressed just as colorfully as the women in the tent were playing the steel drums, guitar, and some kind of maracas.

A woman dressed in a beautiful white peasant blouse with red silk ribbon along the neckline that matched the bright red and orange in her patterned skirt and headscarf greeted them and showed them to a table near the back, facing the water.

As wine and dinner were served, Ben regaled her with stories about New York. But not the typical stories Liz would have expected to hear about the famous city, like crowded transit, rude pedestrians, and how expensive everything was.

Instead, he told her about the garden his neighbor had made on the roof of their apartment building, and how the guy had asked everyone on their floor what their favorite vegetable was and promised to plant it next year.

"You would have loved it," he said. "I went up there a couple of times, and Tom had even tried to put up a greenhouse like the one we saw here on the beach. It was just a hodgepodge of old doors and windows bolted together, probably dangerous as hell, but it was great to see all that greenery in a place you don't expect it. I remember wanting to call you and tell you about it."

Obviously, he hadn't done that, and she didn't have to ask why.

Ben described Central Park and talked about the group who'd invited him to join their touch football game and picnic every first Saturday of the month throughout the summer.

"You love football. That must have been fun."

He gave her a funny look. "I didn't actually join in very often."

"Why not?"

"The teams were made up of both guys and girls, mostly couples who ended up making out on blankets under the trees after the picnic lunch."

"Ah." She chuckled. "A little awkward, I guess."

"Exactly. But eventually I found a good place to go to relieve my frustrations." He grinned across the table and took a sip of wine. Not surprisingly, his plate was already clean, while she'd barely touched hers. "There's a decent gym down the street from my apartment."

With a laugh, she remembered his old exercise routine. "Yes, but is the Thai food as good next door as it was at your last gym?" She used to tease him because he'd never been able to pass by the place without stopping in, which was why he had to go to the gym afterward.

"Nope." His grin widened. "But there's a great dim sum place around the corner."

"So, what else did you get up to in New York?" she asked.

The smile on his face hardened just enough for her to notice, and she almost regretted asking.

"I met my father again," he said.

"You did?" She didn't know what to say. Was that a good thing, or…?

"He died two months ago."

"Oh Ben, I'm sorry. I didn't know."

He shook his head. "It's okay, I guess. I got to see him more in the three months before he died than I had in my entire life."

Other than that one time when he'd rambled about his father out of delirium, family had always been kind of off-limits between them, pretty much by mutual agreement. She'd met his mother, and Ben had known the basics about her history, but that was about it, because anything more would have felt like giving him the key to hurting her. After all, family was her biggest vulnerability.

"It must have been hard." Her throat tightened with emotion.

"Not as hard as losing both your parents," he answered with a sympathetic look.

As a teen, she would have agreed. She'd always thought she'd gotten the worst deal because both her parents had never been around even *before* they died. But how must it have felt to know your father was alive and well…and just didn't want to know you?

"I know you told me once that you contacted him when you were younger, but I thought he didn't…"

"Want anything to do with me?" He answered for her with raised eyebrows. "That was true. But one day I answered a knock at my door in New York, and there he was."

"What did you say?" What would she have said to *her* father if he'd lived and come looking for a second chance to be a real dad?

"It was just after Jeffrey Olsen, and I still thought I was responsible. Everything I'd been working for was falling apart around me, and there he was. I got angry." Beth wanted to reach out for his hand, but she didn't dare. She didn't want to take the risk that he would stop talking. "I yelled at him. How dare he show up at that moment, the worst moment of my life, when I'd spent *years* working my ass off so that when I finally faced him again, I would be the one in control? I would be the one with the ability to turn *him* away without another thought?"

"Did you?"

He looked at her. "No."

She let out a sigh and smiled. She'd been holding her breath without even realizing it. "What did you say to him?"

"He did most of the talking that day, and when he came back, the next day, too. It turned out he was very sick, and he wanted to tell me how much he regretted the way he'd acted the last time we met. I think he regretted a lot of things about his life."

"Did you forgive him?"

"I'm still not sure," he murmured, staring down as his fingers played with the stem of his wineglass. "But when his nurse called me a few weeks later to say that it was time and he was asking for me…I went."

Tears burned the backs of her eyes, and her heart ached for what he'd been through.

She finally reached across the table to squeeze his hand. "I'm glad that you got the chance to know your father better before it was too late, and I'm sure he really appreciated it too."

All that time, she'd been so blind. Thinking only of

how Ben kissing her and moving to New York had ruined everything for *her*.

"It took a lot of guts and heart to take a risk like that." She grimaced and swallowed a sip of wine. "Sorry, does that sound condescending?"

He laughed and cleared his throat, looking over the flower arrangement on the table between them and into her eyes. "Probably not as condescending as me telling you how proud I was of you this afternoon. You had that room full of engineers and marketing geeks clinging to your every word."

As far as subject changes went, she couldn't fault him for giving it a shot, and from that point forward they stuck to safer topics. She dared him to guess which of their old schoolmates was now in jail, and he made her howl with laughter with his reasons why each of them might have ended up in trouble with the law.

Once the plates had been cleared from most of the tables and more drinks had been delivered, the show was ready to begin. From their spot near the edge of the tent, it was a little harder to see the stage, and Ben's back was toward it, so he shifted around the table to sit right beside her.

Part of her wanted him to put his arm around her shoulder and press in closer so she would be able to feel his hard body against hers, but that wouldn't be very professional here, when the dining tent was more than half filled with other convention attendees—and probably her own brother, although she hadn't seen him yet.

Not to mention, she didn't need for him to touch her physically when his body practically hummed beside her, throwing off sexual tension like a live wire, and she knew they were both thinking about it.

And then he took her hand, pulling it beneath the table onto his lap. She glanced up at him with wide eyes, but he shook his head. "The show is starting," he whispered with a devilish grin.

Her breathing hitched as she faced forward again, but every molecule of her being was focused on Ben. On his fingers entwined with hers and the feel of his muscled leg under her palm.

The men and women who had been their servers were now filing onto the stage. Liz loved the multi-colored, flared skirts of the female dancers, but it was difficult to give them the attention they deserved because Ben was driving her crazy. As the booming drums started a heavy, vibrant beat, he moved his hand to her bare knee. In this seated position, her short skirt was already stretched halfway up to her thighs, and she sucked in a breath as she wondered just how daring he would get.

They were well hidden. The beach was at their backs and everyone else was looking toward the stage and nowhere near the two of them. Nevertheless, it felt supremely racy for him to touch her like this in such a public place.

She sucked in a breath as his fingers slipped between her knees, forcing them open just enough for him to shift his palm a little higher. She felt boneless and wound up at the same time.

When he found the silk covering her, he had to know exactly how wet he'd made her. "Please," she whispered.

"Let's get out of here." He took her hand and pulled her from the table, and they ducked out the side of the open tent.

She kicked off her shoes, and he pulled her along into

the night, stopping when they came across the same little greenhouse as before. Or maybe there was more than one. She had no idea and didn't care because Ben was already kissing her. Kissing her like she was water, and he'd spent countless days in the desert.

They crashed into the little glass door of the greenhouse and pushed their way inside. He buried his fist into her hair. They knocked over a potted geranium on the floor. Liz dropped her shoes and pulled at the buttons of his jacket feverishly. She shoved it down his arms. It fell somewhere onto the ground. Considering the floor was littered with soil and plants and sand, she felt bad, until they careened into the potter's bench and Ben shoved whatever happened to be laying there aside and lifted her onto it. Then she didn't care about anything except getting his shirt off.

She fumbled with his belt buckle. He pushed her skirt to her waist and settled between her legs.

She took gasping breaths whenever he let her, filling her lungs with the heady perfume of all different kinds of flowers before everything was snuffed out again and she felt and smelled and tasted only him.

She clutched his head as he trailed hot, wet kisses down the low cut neckline of her dress. "I can't believe we're doing this. I'm not the kind of woman who does this. It's crazy and reckless, and—"

"And you should do it more often. It looks good on you. I've wanted to do this all day and all night," he groaned, slipping the thin straps off her shoulders and revealing her breasts to the torture of his lips and tongue. "The only crazy part is how long I was able to stand beside you in that seminar this afternoon, and then sit across from you at dinner, and go with*out* touching you."

She tipped her head back and hissed as he rolled her nipple between his teeth. "Yes. Oh God, yes."

She heard the telltale sound of a foil wrapper being torn open, and her breathing hitched with expectation and excitement. His hands went to her waist and tugged her closer to the edge of the bench. "My thong," she reminded him.

"Don't worry, I haven't forgotten," he murmured against her lips, urging her to open for him. His tongue swept inside her mouth as his hand slipped between her legs. She thought he would tug them off, but he only moved the scrap of silk aside, baring her just enough to get the job done. It felt deliciously naughty.

The bench was just a little too tall, and so he pulled her off it, right on top of him, filling her so deep so quickly that she cried out.

"Keep your legs tight around my waist and hold on," he rasped in a strained voice. He bent her back over his arm, which itself was braced against the bench, keeping the hard edge from digging into her back.

The two of them were like a hurricane rolling in off the ocean, getting stronger and stronger as it closed in on the shore. Liz was swept away by the strength and power of it, shuddering with every spasm that rocked her from the inside out.

Ben held her tight against his body, and she swore she could hear his heart pounding so loud it echoed in the greenhouse. Then she realized it must have finally started raining. She was hearing the water droplets bouncing off the glass rooftop.

When he set her gently on her feet, she wobbled on jelly legs and grabbed onto his arms.

He looked down at her with a knowing, very male, very self-satisfied grin and pulled her against him once more, leaning over to plant a hard kiss on her still-tender lips. It was too much. She felt too much, and it terrified her.

"You were right, that was maybe a little crazy," he murmured. "But I happen to think being crazy with you is pretty fucking awesome."

He kissed her again, nuzzled her neck. His arms came around her, and he rubbed a circle into the center of her spine with one hand, while the other splayed open between her shoulder blades. "I don't want to let you go yet."

Warmth spread through her. She felt the same, like she could stay here forever with him, cocooned by the pouring rain, the scent of roses, and the shadows of night. It was perfect.

But perfect couldn't last, and neither could the night.

She had to get out now, before she got in any deeper, before her fears swallowed her whole. She hated feeling that way, and with Ben it was sharp and strong.

"You have to," she murmured, feeling suddenly bereft when he stilled, then moved away. "I'm so sorry, Ben, but I'm not the person you think I am. I can't do this. It's too hard. I've got too much baggage for me to ever trust you, trust the two of us together."

"You're afraid," he said simply.

"I'm going back to Seattle."

She glanced up at the glass ceiling. Perfect couldn't last, but the rain might be here to stay for a while.

Chapter Fifteen

"I guess we should go," said Liz. They had readjusted their clothing and tried to tidy up the mess they'd made of the potting bench.

Ben peered through the window. The high wind slashed the rain across the glass. "It's coming down pretty hard."

They raced up the beach. All the torches surrounding the tent had been extinguished and the area was deserted. A corner of the canvas had come loose of its post and flapped in the wind. They kept going and stopped just inside the doors of the resort, dripping water onto the marble floor. Liz shook her arms, but it didn't do any good.

They started for the elevators, hand in hand, and Liz didn't even care what anyone would think if they saw.

Just as Ben pushed the button for the elevator, someone called her name. She turned and looked. It sounded like Daniel, but she didn't see him.

"Liz, wait!"

It was Daniel. He walked toward her from the front desk. He pulled a rolling suitcase behind him with one hand and had his laptop bag thrown over his other shoulder.

His hair was sticking up as if he'd been running his hands through it, and as he got closer, she noticed the dark circles under his eyes had deepened. Behind her, the elevator door slid open and then shut again as she and Ben waited for Daniel to reach them.

She dropped Ben's hand and stepped forward. "Did something happen? What's the matter? You're not leaving, are you?"

"Hey, can we talk for a minute?" He glanced at Ben with a tight expression.

"Yes, of course." She turned to Ben. "I'm sorry, I—"

He shook his head and pushed the button for the elevator again. "Don't worry. Go and do what you need to do."

The elevator door opened, and he stepped inside, leaving her with Daniel.

Liz tilted her head back and looked her brother over, trying to tone down her worried sister face. "I think it's past time we had a real talk. Come on upstairs with me."

He glanced down at his watch, lips pressed together in a thin line, and nodded. "Yeah, okay."

She took his laptop bag and threw it over her shoulder, hooking her other arm through his and pushing the elevator button again. She had this irrational fear that if she didn't hold onto him, Daniel would disappear and be gone forever.

They didn't talk during the ride to her floor, thanks to a couple of convention attendees who'd hopped in with them at the last minute. They gave Liz's bedraggled appearance an interested look. She crossed her arms over her wet bosom, so they started arguing the ethics of logic bombs and trap door programming as necessary industry protection until Liz and Daniel exited on the third floor.

He was quiet. Too quiet.

He left his suitcase at the door and sat down on the edge of her bed.

"What's going on, Daniel? I thought you were having dinner with Laura tonight."

He didn't answer.

She let out a frustrated breath. "You're going to have to talk to me sometime, you know. Is it the poker game? If you feel you have to leave in order to avoid it, I understand."

He turned away from her with a muttered oath.

"Damn it. Did you already get sucked in, is that it?" she asked, her chest tight with worry as she reached out to touch his arm.

He jerked away and laughed. A harsh, choked sound that didn't sound the least bit amused. "The little game going on downstairs is nothing, Liz. Nothing compared to—"

"What? Nothing compared to *what*?" Nervousness had her twisting her hands together. "You're freaking me out now."

"I met with Diego Vargas last night," he said.

The switch in topics threw her off guard. "Yes, you mentioned that earlier." This wasn't about the gambling, but about *Vargas*? Maybe Vargas had made his decision and planned to invest in Ben's company, and Daniel felt guilty?

"Did something go wrong? Does he not want to make a deal with us?" She hurried to relieve his mind. "It's okay, we knew that there was a good possibility he'd decide to go with Optimus Inc."

He took a deep breath. "That's not it. Vargas is more than willing to take a chance on Sharkston. In fact, I've already got his promise on it."

"You do? He is?" Her voice was thin and weak, and there was a heavy thumping in her ears. Her pounding heart. She cleared her throat. "Then what's the problem?" Because it was more than obvious that he wasn't telling her the whole story.

Finally he looked at her. His cheeks were flushed and his lips pulled tight together. "I had to do it, Liz."

"Had to do...*what?*"

"You don't have to worry, I made an amazing deal for us, and I barely had to talk him into it. After he'd looked over the material you emailed to him, he was chomping at the bit to buy us out."

"I don't under—*Buy us out?*" Oh no. *No. No. No.* This couldn't be happening. "We talked about this. I made it very clear in my discussions that we were looking for an investment of venture capital from his company. I have no intention of letting him buy anything. Where the hell did he get the idea that Sharkston Co. is for sale?"

"From me. Because I suggested it."

She was speechless. She couldn't understand why Daniel would have done such a thing.

"Liz, I couldn't take the chance that he would decide to go with Optimus Inc." He pleaded with her to understand. "But when I offered him everything, he couldn't turn it down, and he's willing to pay through the nose for it." He was so animated, as if by faking excitement, she would get excited along with him and forget about the fact that he'd gone behind her back.

She didn't say anything, she couldn't. Her throat was swollen shut. Finally, he stuffed his hands in his pants pockets and lifted his shoulders. "It's money we could really use right now."

And there it was. The real reason for this betrayal. The elephant in the room. "How much?" Her stomach was doing acrobatic rolls and her heart hurt.

"He said he'll give us—"

"No, not Vargas," she snapped, clenching her eyes shut to keep the tears from gathering. "How much do you *owe*, Daniel? How much is it going to cost me to bail you out of trouble? How many years of my life? How much of my work?"

He took a deep breath. "Two hundred grand."

Her whole body shook, and she couldn't breathe. She blinked up at him. He stood there with his mouth hanging open, looking at her like he was the one betrayed and she was losing her mind.

"Liz—"

"I can't. I can't keep doing it." Tears pooled in her eyes until it was like looking through a soda bottle. "You're the only family I've got left, and I've tried so hard. I want to be there for you, but I can't keep fixing your mistakes."

"Hey, just chill. I don't understand what your problem is." He tried to laugh it off and pretend the two of them weren't on the verge of imploding, but it was a thin attempt. "Vargas's company is going to buy out Sharkston for $1.2 *million*, Liz. I've made us more money this way than we could have earned trying to run Sharkston on our own, you know that. With this kind of payout, there'll be plenty to go around. We'll never have to worry about cash again. From my share I'll pay off my debt, and I could even pay you back everything you've given me over the years. You could do anything you want with it. You've had such a good time the last few days, if you wanted to, you could come to Antigua once a month."

He took a half-step toward her. She shook her head and backed away. He didn't understand anything. "You have no idea what I want. All you think about is yourself."

"I screwed up, I admit it." He sounded so wounded, as if losing two hundred thousand dollars was just a small thing, and he should be commended for trying to rectify the problem himself. She wanted to scream. "But I didn't want you to feel like you had to save me again, and part of this company is mine, too. I'm entitled to my share."

"*Your share?*" She couldn't believe what she was hearing.

"And I knew you'd want to keep working," he continued gamely, "so Vargas said as part of the deal he would be willing to have you stay on. The salary would be phenomenal, and you would be a VP in a multi-national corporation, in charge of an entire division devoted to our program. You could still run the whole show, control everything. At the same time, we'll get the cash. His company will bring services and experience to the table that we needed anyway, and—"

"Stop. Just…shut up." She pressed her hands over her ears, blocking him out. She couldn't hear anymore or she was going to lose it completely. "Damn it. You had no right to do this behind my back. None."

"Liz—"

She snapped her hand up to stop him from saying another word. "Forget it. Forget the whole thing. I won't agree to this, and you can be the one to explain the reason why to Vargas."

She turned away and saw his suitcase and his laptop bag. "You were going to leave, weren't you?" She spun around and glared up at him. "You were going to set all this up and then just take off without even explaining it to me."

"I was going to talk to you earlier today when I saw you in the bar, but you seemed so happy after your seminar, and I didn't want to ruin it for you."

"Yeah, that was really thoughtful of you. Thanks," she said sarcastically, then threw her hands up in frustration. "Didn't you think I would talk to Diego and find out what was going on?"

"He has to leave Antigua first thing in the morning anyway, so I didn't think you'd have a chance. When you got back to Seattle, I figured I would have more time to explain everything." Daniel's face crumpled. Gone was the fake optimism and certainty. "They're going to kill me, Liz."

She scoffed and crossed her arms. "Don't be so dramatic."

He stepped toward her. She caught a sheen of moisture in his eyes. "I had a month to pay them back, and at first I was optimistic that we could negotiate an investment contract quickly enough to work something out. But when Laura said that you and Harrison had agreed to this special feature for the balance of the convention, I knew any deal we could make would be delayed."

He took her hand. "These are bad people, Liz. I never should have gotten involved with them, and I know better for next time. But right now I have to do something." His desperation was starting to show. His hands were clammy and he had a frenzied look in his eyes. "They are very serious about hurting me if I can't pay them within the next forty-two hours."

"Forty-two hours?" She started to shake. "Jesus, Daniel. How could you be so stupid?"

"It will never happen again," he promised quickly.

She barked out laughter at the ridiculousness of that. "Even if we went through with this deal, you still can't get two hundred thousand dollars in forty-two hours. It will take weeks to hash out a contract."

"I negotiated a good-faith advance from Vargas. I already have the money."

She felt like the oxygen had been knocked right out of her. If he'd taken money from Vargas then he'd as good as locked her in. How could she back out of this mess without the money to pay him back?

She had to get out of here, away from Daniel. She scrabbled to pull open the door, stumbling out into the hall and heading blindly for the elevators until she saw the red exit sign over the door to the emergency stairwell and changed direction.

"Wait, where are you going?" His voice followed her, but she didn't stop. Couldn't stop.

The sound of her broken sobs bounced back at her off the cement walls as she took the steps at a run. Halfway to the next level, she tripped and kept herself from tumbling all the way down the hard steps by the skin of her teeth and a hard grip on the handrail.

She gave up. Collapsing onto the step with her knees drawn up to her chin, she gave up.

Chapter Sixteen

Ben looked at his watch. It was almost midnight, but he wouldn't sleep tonight. He couldn't stop thinking about Beth and the things that were still unsaid between them, but it didn't matter. The reality was, she was too stubborn to let go of her past…and he was never getting her out of his system.

He thought about calling her, to find out why her brother had looked so troubled. There was definitely something going on there, but it was a family thing and not his place to intrude when she obviously didn't need him.

Wired and restless, he worked for an hour on the computer, but he still couldn't settle and so finally he decided to find Nolan and Meredith at the bar. On his way down, he changed his mind about Beth and stopped at the front desk. "Do you think you could ring room 304 for me?"

She picked up the phone and punched in the number. After a moment, she shook her head and hung up. "I'm sorry, sir, but there's no answer. Would you like me to leave a message?"

"No, that's okay."

He remembered the suitcase her brother had been carrying, but Beth wouldn't have left with Daniel, not without at least saying good-bye, would she?

He didn't think either of them could have gotten out of here anyway, even if that had been the plan. The weather had taken a turn for the worse. Since dinner, the winds had picked up considerably and the rain was still pounding down outside. It was so bad, the fury of the storm could be heard from within the hotel and every once in a while people stopped and looked worriedly at one another.

The likelihood that the wind and rain could damage the actual hotel and put anyone in any real danger was slim, but guests were being asked not to venture outside from now until the storm had run its course.

Entering the bar, he looked around. The doors to the outdoor patio were shut tight this evening and the air conditioning and other non-essential electrical services had been also been cut for safety reasons, so the space was hot and muggy. That hadn't kept people from piling in on top of one another. The bar was packed. Since the convention had technically ended today, except for the closing luncheon tomorrow afternoon, it was now party time, and everyone wanted to let loose a little bit.

He didn't see Beth, but as he turned to leave he spotted Nolan and Meredith sitting together with Diego Vargas at a small table.

Jemarcho's President and CEO stood and greeted him with a smile, shaking his hand. He was a tall, good looking man. Because of his global success with Jemarcho, he'd had the misfortune to be featured in the news almost as often as Ben and Nolan had been recently, but especially during his divorce last year.

It was a no brainer that partnering with Jemarcho was the best option for Optimus Inc. Ben had come to Antigua knowing that and being determined to get it done, but he found himself hesitating now. Beth needed that investment money just as much as he did. It shouldn't matter, they had both agreed that their business choices would be kept separate from their personal choices, and yet he didn't want to hurt her.

They saw him and waved him over. "It's nice to see you again. Have you been enjoying the convention?" he asked Vargas.

Diego glanced down at a smiling Meredith. "Now that I've been introduced to your lovely friend, I'm having a *much* better time," he said.

Ben lifted a narrowed gaze at Nolan. *That* wasn't the way he wanted to do business.

Meredith saw his look and punched him in the arm. "Oh good God, get your mind out of the gutter. Since the two of you have basically deserted me here, I was at the bar yesterday *by myself*, and Diego took pity on me and introduced himself."

She took that moment to get up. "I'm going to brave the crowds for another drink. Does anyone else want one?"

Ben and Nolan declined. Diego still had a half-full beer, but he stood with her. "I will accompany you," he said.

"I'm quite capable of going alone." She patted his shoulder and smiled. "Besides, I have a feeling the discussion is about to get technical and boringly businesslike, so I had better fortify myself."

As Meredith weaved her way toward the bar, Vargas clasped his hands on the table in front of him. "Listen Ben, I've heard some distressing information about you recently."

Ben frowned, surprised. "What kind of information?"

"What part did you play in that sad business surrounding Jeffrey Olsen's death?"

Shock slowed his reaction, and Steve opened his mouth to respond, but Ben held up his hand. He looked right at Vargas. "Olsen was my first business partner, but it wasn't a good match. We didn't see eye-to-eye on a number of things, so I called it quits before we got in too deep, and we went our separate ways."

"Is it true that he killed himself because you defamed his reputation and left him high and dry with no assets and no prospects?"

Nolan shot forward. "Who the hell is spreading this horseshit?"

Diego's eyebrows lifted. "So it's not true?"

Ben shrugged. "I suppose that depends on whose viewpoint you're looking at it from," he said, resigned.

"What the hell are you talking about?" Nolan snapped at Ben before turning to Diego. "As sad as Jeffrey Olsen's death was, everyone knows that he screwed Ben over after betraying every other business connection he'd ever made. Olsen was on a slippery downhill slope, and Ben had no choice but to get out when he did or risk going down with him. If the man felt isolated enough after all that to take his own life, no one else should have to bear the burden of that decision."

"It's not as simple as that," Ben argued.

Diego shook his head. "No, your partner is right. I think

it probably is that simple. After hearing of this incident, I looked into it on my own, and it seems to have gone down pretty much as you've described."

"Then why did you ask me about it?"

"I always get as many points of view as I can before making up my mind on something." He crossed his arms and looked back and forth between Ben and Nolan. "Listen, there's something else we should talk about. I know we've already discussed an investment contract between our companies, but I don't know if I can do that for you anymore."

Ben was disappointed, but part of him was also proud because it meant that Beth must have wowed Diego with her proposal.

Nolan leaned forward. "Is it because of those rumors? Because you just said—"

"No, this is purely a business decision," Diego assured them. "I shouldn't tell you the details, but given our previous negotiations, I probably owe you a bit of an explanation. The truth is I'm buying out a company in order to develop a very similar product. Because of the potential for conflicts of interest, I wouldn't be able to handle your contract at the same time." He sat back and took a swig from his beer.

He was being discreet, but everyone knew that the "very similar product" had to be the one Beth's company had been working on.

"Well, I can certainly understand where you're coming from. It sounds like a fantastic opportunity." Something about this didn't sound right. "But I was under the impression that Sharkston was looking for investment capital, not someone to buy them outright."

Now that Ben had put all the cards on the table, Diego

stopped beating around the bush. "You're right. That's what I thought, too, but apparently their circumstances have changed. When I talked to her partner, he admitted they're hard-up for cash, and they're looking to make a different sort of deal." He shrugged. "The opportunity is too appealing to pass up, even if I'm reluctant to do business with people like them."

People like them? Beth was one of the most honorable, hard-working people he'd ever known. Diego should count his lucky stars to be doing business with—

"It was her?" said Nolan, surprised. "Elizabeth Carlson was the one who went to you with stories about Ben and Jeffrey Olsen?"

"An anonymous, handwritten note was slipped under my hotel room door."

Ben dismissed it right away, but Nolan wasn't letting it go.

"It had to be her. I assume she was trying to sway your decision, because she knew you were leaning in our favor?" Nolan shook his head in disgust. "I hadn't pegged that woman as the type of person to try something like that."

"The only thing those rumors have swayed is my decision on whether or not Ms. Carlson will become my vice president as part of the deal. I don't think I want her working in my company."

"She wouldn't—" Ben started, but he had to admit it was possible for Beth to have spilled the beans about Olsen. Ben hadn't told anyone else about what happened.

With pinched brows Vargas leaned forward. "Ben, I know we had discussions of our own, and I apologize for changing the game at the last minute. I don't appreciate these kinds of tactics, so despite the opportunity, if you can give me a reason not to do business with these people…"

"I'm not playing those kinds of games with you, Diego," he told the other man, even as his stomach turned at the idea that Beth had taken the opportunity to do the same to him. Deep down, he knew she wouldn't. And even though she'd broken his heart not once, but twice, he still had to do what was right. For her. Even if it meant doubling his failures all in one night. "The truth is, Elizabeth Carlson is smart, dedicated, and you'd probably be a fool to pass up the chance to work with her."

Nolan snorted. "Are you kidding me? After what she's done you're going to sit there and extoll her virtues?" He leaned in to growl in Ben's ear. "Is the sex *that* fucking good?"

Ben snarled at him. "Shut the hell up."

Diego drummed his fingers on the table. "I don't think I understand all that's going on here."

"Neither do I, but this buyout arrangement you've described doesn't sound right," Ben warned. In fact, it sounded like the desperate actions of someone who needed money, fast. If Beth had been that desperate, why hadn't she said anything to him?

"I've already got a deal, and I've paid in advance to make certain it stands until the contracts can be drawn up," Vargas insisted. Ben was surprised to hear that too. She'd actually taken money before the deal could be put in writing? The whole thing smacked of bad business practice, and that didn't sound like her.

Diego's jaw clenched. "If either of you know something that might change my mind enough to call this whole thing off before my check gets cashed, tell me now."

This was something he could swing to his advantage. With just a few words about Daniel's gambling problems, he might be able to convince Vargas that having anything to do with Sharkston Co. was a bad idea. Diego would be signing on the dotted line for Optimus Inc. instead before they were even finished their drinks.

Maybe a few months ago he would have done it, but today he understood something he hadn't then. The saying, "just business" was bullshit. There was no such thing as just business. Every action was personal. Every decision could hurt. And even now, the last person he wanted to hurt was Beth.

"Ben?" Nolan looked at him expectantly, but Ben shook his head.

He caught sight of a figure across the crowded room. He stood and glanced down at Diego. "I'm sorry, but I've got to go."

Diego sat back, looking a little disappointed. "If that's your position."

Nolan let out a snort of disgust, but Ben ignored him.

"Whatever happens," he said to Diego. "I think you should give Elizabeth Carlson a chance. You won't regret working with her."

The man tilted his head with raised eyebrows. "I certainly wasn't expecting Ben Harrison to give me the soft-sell for someone else's contract. Are you sure *you* don't work for Sharkston?"

"I just know a good thing when I see it, even if it isn't mine." He turned to leave, having noticed his target slipping out of the bar. "I'm sorry, but I see someone I have to talk to."

He ignored Nolan's objection and threw some cash on the table for the drinks. He kept his eye on Daniel as the man headed for the elevators. What the hell was going on?

Ben caught up just as the door was sliding closed and inserted his foot into the track. Once it had slowly re-opened, he leaned his shoulder against it and crossed his arms.

"Daniel Carlson," he said in a hard voice, looking the thin, disheveled man up and down with a grimace. He looked a wreck. "What the hell have you and your sister been up to?"

"Sorry to disappoint you, Harrison," Daniel snapped. "But I don't have time for this." He stabbed the elevator button, trying to force the door to close, and swore when it wouldn't.

Ben reached in and grabbed the guy by the scruff of the neck, dragging him out into the lobby. "You're going to make time," he growled. A possibility suddenly occurred to him and he added, "Because I have a feeling you're trying to screw over your own sister. Does she even know what you've been up to?"

He looked up sharply, giving credence to Ben's suspicion. "What the hell do you care, anyway? You're the competition."

"Answer me before I beat the truth out of you."

"Go to hell." Daniel shoved Ben's hands off him, but then he hesitated and seemed to deflate. "She knows now," he finally admitted.

It didn't explain how Diego had found out about Jeffrey Olsen, but he was pretty sure that Beth hadn't been the one to make that ridiculous deal. It had been Daniel, probably acting behind her back.

The man's brows drew together, and he bit his lip. His

shoulders drooped. "She didn't take it well."

Ben sneered. "Did you honestly think she would? Even I know she would never agree to sell Sharkston. What the hell were you thinking?"

Daniel looked up. His eyes were dark with worry. Something else was wrong.

"What is it?" Ben's stomach clenched.

"I haven't seen her since I told her about the deal." He glanced out the large windows into the darkness. The wind whistled and the glass was pelted with rain. "She took off and hasn't returned to her room. It's been a few hours, and I can't find her anywhere."

Chapter Seventeen

Daniel spilled the whole story while he and Ben performed a systematic search of the entire resort. First they'd gone back to the bar and gotten Nolan, Meredith, and Diego to help. Everyone was taking a different wing of the hotel, but Ben wasn't letting Daniel out of his sight and kept him close.

An hour and a half later, Ben knew more than he ever wanted to know about the low-lifes Beth's brother owed money to and what they were going to do to him if he didn't pay up within the next few days.

"What about the note to Vargas about Jeffrey Olsen's death," he demanded.

Daniel hesitated, but Ben moved as if to grab him again, and he jerked back and stammered, "It was me; it was me. A reporter was asking some questions and wanted to know if I knew what had happened with you and Olsen, so I looked it up online and decided to tell Vargas. I was hoping if he thought you were dirty, negotiating with him would be easier."

Ben also knew that despite being a selfish, insensitive, asshole, Daniel did love his sister and he felt horrible about what he'd done. "I'll fix it," he said, not for the first time. Or the fifth. "I just hope she's okay. She has to be okay. Why would she take off like that? Where the hell could she be?"

They'd walked every floor, gone into all the conference rooms and back to the bar. There was only one place they hadn't looked yet—outside on the grounds. Ben turned to Daniel, hiding his own worry by giving orders. "It's time to enlist the staff to help. Go to the front desk and let them know she's missing. I'm going to check outside."

Daniel nodded. Ben left him. After returning to his room for a light jacket he went outside, armed with a flashlight from one of the security guards.

The storm still raged. Rain pelted him, feeling like sheets of needles falling on his face and neck. The wind threatened to lift him right off his feet, but he pressed forward.

He squinted into the darkness. It was impossible to see anything and the beam of his flashlight couldn't penetrate more than two feet in front of him.

"Beth!" The word was carried away on the wind as if he'd never uttered it.

In just fifteen minutes, he was soaked to the bone, and his voice was hoarse from calling her name, but he had a strong feeling she was out here.

In fact…he panned the flashlight in a half-circle over the expanse of beach laid out in front of him again and stopped on the same small greenhouse they'd invaded last night.

A palm tree had fallen on top of it. The trunk was being held up by the steel roof trusses, but it looked as if it would snap them at any moment. He raced to the door, but something inside the greenhouse had fallen in front of it, blocking the way.

"Beth? Beth, are you in there?" There was no answer. He examined the greenhouse walls. Most of the glass was actually still intact, except for the ceiling. He shone the flashlight through the window beside the door, but there wasn't anything in there other than broken pots and spilled dirt.

He was about to keep going and make his way to the beach, when he heard the muffled sound of a moan. It was faint, immediately torn away by the wind—or maybe it was a product of the wind—but he had to be sure.

"Beth!"

He stuffed the flashlight under his arm as he struggled to push the greenhouse door in. Whatever had fallen up against it was tall and heavy and it was positioned at a tilt, like a wedge that prevented him from budging the door. As he shoved, trying to force the barricade back, he heard a sprinkling of glass falling to the ground, and prayed that whatever was left of the roof wasn't getting ready to crash down.

"Beth! Answer me," he called again, fighting the tremor in his voice.

Fuck. If she was in there… If she'd been hurt…

He needed to remain calm. He had to stay in control even as fear like he'd never felt before played havoc with his imagination, sending him gruesome images of her bloody body lying on the floor impaled by long shards of glass. "Oh God, baby. Say something. Let me know you're okay."

Another moan. And then movement, something sliding on the ground, shifting in the broken glass.

"Ben?" Her voice was weak and shaky, but it was Beth. She was definitely inside.

"Hold on, I'm coming." Rain bled into his eyes and down his face, and his feet slid across the wet flagstone step in front of the greenhouse. The structure blocking the other side of the door wavered as he shoved harder, and he had to force himself to ease up, go slowly. He needed to slide it across the floor, but he didn't want to send it tipping over when he wasn't sure where Beth was.

Finally, there was room to get the door open enough to slip through. He swiped a hand across his face and got down on his knees to duck under the blockage. It turned out to be a toppled shelving unit. He edged inside and swung the flashlight on the space in front of him, but saw nothing besides a mess of mangled plants and broken glass spilled in dirty rain puddles, until he got to the corner of the greenhouse.

"Shit." He smacked his forehead off the rim of a flower pot still hanging from the ceiling as he hastened forward. Beth lay on the ground, struggling to sit up. Blood trickled down the side of her face, and she was soaking wet.

"Are you all right? What happened?" He crouched on one knee beside her and pointed the flashlight in her face. She squinted against the shine and tried to lift her hand in front of her eyes, but he stopped her. "No, just let me have a look at you."

"I'm fine," she insisted in a stronger voice, but her hand fell back down to her side and she let him cup her chin in his hand to take a look. "I fell and knocked myself on the head when the tree came down through the roof," she muttered.

"There's glass everywhere. Did it cut you?" He smoothed

the hair from her forehead to examine the gash in her temple. There was a bump there, too. The rain made the blood run down her face, but he didn't think she was actually bleeding anymore. Still, with head injuries you could never be sure. He needed to get her to the infirmary.

"I was in here feeling sorry for myself and not paying any attention to how bad the storm was getting. Suddenly, all I heard was a crash. The glass from the roof missed me, but that cabinet over there came out of nowhere and attacked me." She forced a smile.

He glanced back over his shoulder at the structure that had tried to keep him out, thinking how heavy it had been while he was trying to shove it out from in front of the door.

"*Jesus.* You're lucky that thing didn't crush you flat." His stomach churned, and he turned back. She was pale, her lips pulled into a tight line. "Are you hurt anywhere else?" he asked.

She started to roll her shoulder but let out a hiss of pain and grabbed her elbow, holding her arm in close to her body. "I think I might have wrenched something."

When he examined her further, he also discovered a pretty deep cut in her right calf, but he decided it was safer to move her than stay here. He put the flashlight in her lap and slipped his arms beneath her, carefully lifting her off the ground. "Let's get you back inside before you freeze to death," he said.

At the door of the greenhouse, he put her on her feet and helped her duck down to get through before following her out. She was able to stand on her own, but the winds were still strong, and the rain pelted them both.

He gathered her back up into his arms. "You don't have to do that," she protested.

"Don't argue with me." He frowned, jaw clenched as he started walking back in the direction of the hotel. The fear that had gripped him from the moment Daniel had said she was missing was not a feeling that he liked. "I'm not in the mood."

"What's the matter?" she asked.

"You disappear in the middle of a hurricane and have the nerve to ask what's the matter?"

"It's not a hurricane, and I didn't—"

He glared down at her until she shut up. "Do you know what that did to me? To find you in there? That tree could have come right down...the glass could have cut an artery. What if you had a concussion and nobody found you out here before you bled out, or what if you never regained consciousness? *Fuck, Beth*," he snarled, frustration pounding in his temples. He could almost always find a way to charm himself out of a situation, but this fear was immobilizing. He didn't know how to handle it. "Damn it. You could have been killed."

She lifted a hand to his cheek, looking up at him with wide eyes. "Stop," she whispered. He snapped his mouth shut, but that apparently wasn't what she meant. "No. *Stop*. Stop walking. Put me down." She slapped his wet shoulder with a light fist.

"Don't be ridiculous. I'm taking you inside to find a doctor." He kept walking until she started hitting him more determinedly. Finally, he did what she asked even though he had to hold her steady.

"What is wrong with you?" he growled, watching her weave on her feet.

"What are you saying?"

"What do you mean?" He waved an arm toward the lights of the resort ahead of them. "I'm saying we need to get you out of the damn storm."

"No, the other thing." She pulled away and peered up at him through the rain as if trying to find whatever answer she was asking for in his face. "Why? Why did you come looking for me?"

"Did that shelving unit addle your brains? Of course I came looking for you. I was worried."

Her brows drew together and she shook her head. "I'm sure my brother was worried, too, and maybe a few other people, but none of them are here yelling at me."

All the hope and fear she'd stuffed down his throat the last few days bubbled over in a rush of emotion.

"Damn it, Beth!" he yelled over the pounding rain. "You can't stroll back into my life after rejecting everything I had to give, make me fall for you...*again*...and then just disappear like that! I won't do this again with someone who doesn't feel the same way."

He watched her go still, like a deer caught in the headlights. He waited for her to tell him she cared too, but she dropped her head so he couldn't see her face.

He understood. Fear was a powerful motivator, and Beth had more reason than most to want to protect herself from loss. But she had to see that he was as sure a thing as she was ever likely to find.

As the moments ticked by in time with his thumping heart beats and she didn't say anything, he swallowed his disappointment.

Finally, he let out a long breath and gently pulled her into his side. "Come on," he murmured. "Let's get out of the rain."

He didn't try to carry her again, but lent her the strength of a supportive arm so she could walk on her own.

Chapter Eighteen

The next morning, Liz lay in bed. She was clean, dry, and warm, with a thick white bandage taped to her temple and another couple covering the stitches in her leg. Rain still pattered against her window, but the tropical storm had been downgraded, and the rest of it would probably blow away by the end of the day. The airlines were already rescheduling flights off the island.

When she and Ben had returned to the resort and she realized just how many people had been looking for her, she was so embarrassed she couldn't look any of them in the eye. Ben had accompanied her to her room and helped her get into bed. Then he'd simply called for the nurse and told her to get some sleep.

She hadn't said anything to him at all. Not since his confession out in the rain, or when the nurse had arrived and he'd discretely left the room without a word. Not even when every aching inch of her body had been begging her to call him back.

Daniel had shown up at the door a few minutes ago, but neither of them had much to say to one another. Her disappointment in him was still so close to the surface that she choked up every time she opened her mouth and ended up shaking her head and waving him away again.

Now he came out of the bathroom with a glass of water and approached her bedside.

"Thank you," she said as he handed it to her gently.

He didn't move away. He stood over her like he wanted to say something, but only managed to clear his throat.

"Daniel, stop hovering," she said, feeling more weary and beaten than she'd ever felt. "I'll talk to Diego later today, and we'll finalize the deal. Everything will be fine."

"I've already talked to him," he said. "I told him there'd be no sale, but if he was still willing to talk investment under the terms that had been previously proposed, then Sharkston would be happy to do business with him."

She looked up in surprise, despite the tiny stab of pain that shot through her with the movement. "But what about the money he gave you, the money that you owe?"

"Oh," he continued. "And I'm also tendering my resignation. Do you want me to email it to you?"

"Your resignation? You can't just resign." She struggled to sit up. He quickly moved to help her, readjusting her pillow behind her back. "What did I miss? What the hell is going on?"

He sat down on the edge of the bed, fingers plucking at the down-filled coverlet. "I hope you know that I love you," he said slowly. "It may not seem like it, because I've been such a pathetic, selfish dick, but I know how lucky I am to have you for a sister."

"Daniel." She reached for his hand and opened her mouth to tell him it was okay, but he wasn't finished.

"What I did to you was very wrong. I knew it, Liz. And I still did it anyway. I was weak and afraid, but that's no excuse. I'm done making excuses, and I'm done being weak." His forehead creased. "I want to do more than apologize this time. I want to make it right. I want to make you proud."

"Oh Daniel, I didn't mean what I said yesterday. I'll always be there for you. We can figure it out together. I want to help, you know that."

He nodded. "I know, but that kind of makes it all worse. Just because you're my big sister doesn't mean I can let you take care of me forever. At some point, I have to grow up and be a man." He took a deep breath. "And at some point, you have to let me, so that you can have your own life."

"I have a life," she objected, shifting uncomfortably.

"Really?" He looked at her with skepticism. "I might be self-involved, but I've seen the way you operate."

She jerked her head up in surprise. "How is that?"

"As if life is something you can protect yourself from." He took her hand gently as if she might break. "It's not, you know, not if you're doing it right."

Defensive, she snatched her hand back and said, "This from the guy who might very well get both his legs broken when we get off the plane tomorrow?"

He crossed his arms and grinned. "At least I'm willing to take chances."

"On all the wrong things!" she snapped.

"You're absolutely right," he agreed, "but all that's changed. From now on I want to take the right chances…

with Laura." He looked sheepish and suddenly shy. "I've told her everything, and she's agreed that if I can get myself straightened out and fix my mistakes, she'll give me a chance to be with her."

She didn't know what to say. Tears clogged her throat as she reached over and squeezed *his* hand.

"Aren't you afraid…I mean, what if it doesn't work out between the two of you?" She held her breath.

He lightly chucked her under the chin like she wasn't the older sibling. "Are you asking about me and Laura…or you and Harrison?"

She sputtered, but he was right. "Oh, just shut up," she muttered. "Since when are you actually insightful?"

"It must be the sea water. Don't worry, I'm sure it'll pass," he joked, gently swiping his thumb across her cheek to catch a tear.

"Wait," she said. "How are you going to get the money to pay your gambling debt if you told Diego Vargas the deal was off?"

He squared his shoulders. "I've accepted a new job and negotiated a loan. I'll be paying it back for a long time, with interest. But at least it's a start on the right track." He paused and squeezed her fingers. "And maybe one day you'll be able to forgive me."

"I already do," she whispered. "I forgive you, and I love you." And she was already proud of him. Maybe this is what he needed to finally find himself. "But who gave you a loan and what's this new job?"

"Diego agreed to let me keep the advance he already paid us, but I'm going to work for Jemarcho in order to pay it off."

"He actually went for that? But I don't understand why you have to leave Sharkston. How am I going to run the company without you?" she asked.

"We both know that Sharkston is your baby. It's going to be tough enough to stay on track no matter how determined I am to get it right this time. This is for the best. Becoming nothing but an employee in a big company that isn't run by my sister—who would do anything to bail me out of trouble—will help me be accountable for my own actions."

"Did Ben Harrison have something to do with this?"

"He helped me talk to Vargas," Daniel admitted.

She sputtered. "How dare he—"

Daniel raised his hand. "Don't be angry. He did it for you. When Vargas found out what I had done, he was ready to write off Sharkston completely. He would have signed with Optimus Inc. for sure. But Harrison talked him into giving both of us another chance."

Her mind churned as she processed everything that had happened while she was sleeping. Ben had changed. The man she'd known a year ago would never have blown a career-making business deal for any reason, especially not for…love. Then again, she wondered if she'd ever really known that man, or if she'd only projected all the mistakes her parents had made onto him because he'd been just as driven to succeed.

Had she blown it now too? Thrown away the best thing that had ever happened to her?

Daniel got up from the bed. "I think you two need to talk."

She nodded absently, caught up in her twirling thoughts and boomerang emotions. She looked up when she heard the door click shut. Daniel was gone.

Chapter Nineteen

After Daniel left, Liz kept hoping Ben would come see her, but he didn't. Not that she blamed him after last night, but he wasn't answering his phone, either.

Diego Vargas stopped by though to see if she was feeling better after her adventure in the storm, thankfully after she'd finished dressing and no longer looked like something the cat had dragged in.

"Mr. Vargas, I'm so sorry about what's happened," she started.

He dismissed her apology without even blinking. "It wasn't your doing, and I've already made an arrangement with your brother, so don't waste another thought on it."

"I want to thank you for that. You're being very patient and understanding with Daniel." She narrowed her gaze. Daniel was still family, and protecting him would be a hard habit to break. "Do you mind if I ask why?"

He chuckled at her suspicion. "Do you remember when

I told you about the family business?"

"Your sister's winery? Of course."

"Yes, well. Once there was a brother who should have taken his place in that business too, but he was a hell of a screw up and got himself kicked out of the house at seventeen."

She put her hand to her throat. "You?"

"Me." He grinned. "I've made a lot of mistakes on the way to finding my own path, and I think I understand where your brother is coming from. Perhaps I can help him discover what his path will be."

"Don't go *too* easy on him."

"Of course not," he said with a sparkle in his eye. "Daniel wouldn't learn anything if it was easy."

He said good-bye and turned to leave, but she stopped him at the door. "About your kind offer," she started. "I'm very grateful that you were still willing to consider Sharkston Co. as an investment opportunity, but I can't accept. It wouldn't be right."

"Why do you say so?"

"Because I think if things had progressed without this fiasco, you would have chosen Optimus Inc. to invest in, and I don't want to cheat them out of that opportunity." She twisted her hands together nervously. "Not to mention, they have developed a superior product that will revolutionize the industry, and I don't want to cheat *you* out of the opportunity to be a part of it."

He had a bemused look on his face. "I appreciate the sentiment, Ms. Carlson, but you sell yourself short. Your passion impressed me from the moment we met, and after reviewing your demo package and listening to you speak this week, there was really no question what my decision would be. Although Optimus Inc. has a brilliant business strategy, Sharkston's product is the best match for my company, and I was determined to get my hands on it from the beginning."

"Really?" Her heart sped up.

He nodded. "Really."

Later, she ventured downstairs for the closing luncheon. She noted that the ballot box that had been sitting on the table for the last few days was gone.

She took a deep breath and entered the conference room. Tables and chairs had been set up for the luncheon, and she looked around for a familiar face. Diego Vargas had already left for the airport. She tried to find Ben but didn't see him. She didn't see Steve Nolan or Meredith Stone either.

Finally, she sat down at a table with Daniel, Laura, and Elise, the woman she'd met earlier in the week from MagnaTech, who kept glancing at her and biting her lip as if the curiosity might kill her.

After changing her mind three times, she finally asked Laura where the representatives from Optimus Inc. were.

Laura tsked in dismay. "Apparently, there was some unfortunate incident involving a reporter breaking into Mr. Nolan's room late last night. The brazen woman was ejected from the premises, but Mr. Nolan decided to leave the hotel and stay elsewhere, and I don't blame him."

"And Mr. Harrison?"

"Oh, I don't know," she answered, glancing over her shoulder in surprise. "I didn't receive his regrets. I can't imagine what's keeping him."

Daniel told Laura that Liz shouldn't have to do the speech,

not after what had happened and not alone, but Liz insisted on going ahead with it. She wasn't going to do the short speech she'd prepared the day before about seizing opportunities and making your own destiny, though. That definitely felt fake. Because she was a fake. A fake and a coward.

Laura had warned her that the luncheon would begin with the results of the competition, and the announcement of Tyson Wallace's choice for the yearly endorsement. When Optimus Inc. was declared the winner in what turned out to be a very close vote, Liz clapped loudly. She was relieved. Ben deserved it, and she hoped it helped him get some valuable exposure, especially since he seemed to have given up on Jemarcho.

When the room quieted, Laura, a professional in every way, got up to say a brief thank you on behalf of Optimus Inc., apologizing for both executives' unfortunate absence, and assuring the audience that they were very grateful for the recognition. After that, lunch was served, and then it was time for the speech. She approached the front, but there was still no sign of Ben.

She waited a moment as they called his name once more, and then Laura introduced just her, and Liz decided to go for it anyway. Her smile was shaky as she gazed out into the sea of faces, and she didn't know what to do with her hands. She was nervous in a way she'd never been before, because she'd never risked so much before this moment.

"Good afternoon," she started in a small voice and cleared her throat. "As some of you may know, I'm the president of a tiny little start up with big dreams but no capital." There were a few chuckles at her blunt honesty. "So I arrived on this island with every intention of taking risks and being bold." The door at the back of the hall creaked open and a figure slipped inside.

Ben.

Their gazes met and held. "The trouble was, I had absolutely no idea how to take a real risk because I've lived my entire life in fear. But one person has taught me about real courage these last few days," she continued, her heart pounding as she spoke directly to him. It didn't even matter if no one else understood a word that she was saying.

"He took me swimming with sharks, showed me it was okay to dance in the surf and get a little wet, and even braved a tropical storm for me. It's because of him that I may finally be ready to take the ultimate risk—with my heart."

She sent him a trembling smile, asking wordlessly if he would accept her apology. Chairs turned as others noticed the direction of her gaze…but he had already left the room.

Chapter Twenty

Liz tightened the sash holding her long jacket closed and knocked on the door. She wondered if he was even there, but then she heard the sound of the shower being turned off and knocked again. Louder.

Maybe this wasn't such a good idea, but she was turning over a new leaf as a risk taker, and nothing was going to make her give up on Ben unless he flat out said in no uncertain terms that he didn't want her anymore.

The door opened. Her breath caught. She should have realized that running water could mean he had just been *in the shower*. He wore nothing but a white towel around his hips, and his skin dripped with moisture. Steam wafted from the open bathroom door, and a quick glance inside proved that the mirror was fogged up. "Beth? What are you doing here?"

"Um, can I come in?" she asked. She should leave him alone to…but she couldn't. She didn't want to. It was get this out now, or lose her nerve.

He nodded and stepped aside. She moved forward, inhaling the scent of freshly lathered bar soap on his skin. She had to clench her hands together to keep from reaching for him immediately.

With the door closed, he crossed the room and leaned against the edge of the desk, waiting for her to speak.

She didn't know how to start. "I heard what happened to your partner. Is Steve going to press charges against the reporter for breaking into his room?"

His expression didn't lighten, but he said, "I don't know. I think there's more to the situation than a reporter getting overzealous trying to find a story any way she can."

"Why do you say that?"

He lifted an eyebrow. "Because apparently she was naked when he found her there."

"Oh."

"Yeah."

She nodded and took a deep breath. "Listen, I heard what you did for Daniel and what you said to Diego Vargas. He's agreed to void the sale my brother tried to negotiate and still wants to make an investment deal with Sharkston. And it's all because of you."

He didn't say anything.

"I need to know why you did it. Why would you throw away your best shot for Optimus Inc., just to drag my fool brother out of trouble? Why would you help my company succeed at the expense of your own?"

"I didn't do it for him." He straightened, but didn't come toward her. "After last night, you still don't get it?"

She bit her lip. "I thought business was just business, and

we were going to keep our personal lives out of it."

"That was never going to happen. When it comes to you, it was always going to be personal for me," he admitted, crossing his arms. "Unless there's nothing personal left between us."

Was he saying that was the case now? That she was wasting her time? With a deep breath, she took a step forward, not ready to give up. "You walked out on my speech this afternoon."

He nodded, his gaze inscrutable. "Yes."

She took another step and stopped right in front of him. "It was a good speech. All about learning to take risks and trusting your heart."

"Is that all you came here to say?" His voice didn't soften an iota.

"No, I just figured I'd start with that." She sighed. "I wanted to tell you that no matter how I felt, I never would have agreed to go to New York with you."

He squared his shoulders. "Well, that's that then, isn't it? Maybe you should leave. I've got a plane to—"

"No, wait. This isn't coming out right," she interrupted, shaking her head. "It's the truth, but…only because I think I needed this year to be on my own. I needed the challenge of starting my own business, and to work things out with my brother. I needed to face the truth if I was ever going to be able to look to the future, and the truth is, it's hard to imagine being with you and not think of how much it would hurt to lose you. In fact, it's impossible to imagine being with you, without worrying that our love would one day turn stale and cold, just like my parents' marriage."

She dared a glance at his face. He looked down his nose like she was nothing to him. The dagger she'd stabbed herself with when she pushed him away stuck into her heart a little deeper. Still, she was on a roll and wouldn't stop until she'd at least said everything she came here to say. She deserved nothing, but Ben, at least, deserved the truth.

But she couldn't see that look in his eyes when she said it, and so she glanced down at the floor. "I spent the last few days telling myself that we would just have some fun together and then go our separate ways at the end of the week. I thought it would be easy. At least way easier than admitting I've been in love with you all this time."

Her fingers twisted in the folds of her jacket. She needed to get through this. "But I realized that even if this thing between us lasts only one day, I'll take it. I'll take as much time with you as I'm given because the alternative is to let you walk away again…and I just can't seem to do that."

"You don't have much choice anymore," he said coldly. "I laid my soul bare and offered you everything that it was in me to give, not once, but twice. Do you really think I'll do that a third time?"

"I was hoping…"

He didn't say anything. He didn't smile and say it was all right, that they could have one more chance. He just watched her until she wanted to crawl down into the floor and disappear.

She swallowed and nodded, her movements jerky. "Okay. I…I understand," she whispered, feeling like her chest had been cracked open and her heart ripped out. "My fault. I realized my mistake too late, and you have every right to walk…"

She couldn't finish. She spun around, fumbling through her tears to find the door knob. She yanked it open and stumbled out into the hallway.

Somehow, she made it to the elevator and jabbed her finger on the button. It seemed to take forever, but when the door opened, she rushed inside.

"What floor?"

Startled, she conspicuously swiped the tears from her cheeks and realized she wasn't alone. There were three men and two women in the elevator with her. *Just my luck.* She groaned inwardly. A quick glance confirmed they were *all* part of the convention, with badges still hanging from their necks.

"Sorry?" she croaked.

"What. Floor?" The man closest to the keypad repeated impatiently. One of the women jabbed him sharply in the arm.

"Um." She obviously hadn't been thinking when she raced down the hall. Her room was right beside Ben's, but she couldn't go back there. She just couldn't.

"Wherever you're going is fine." The elevator door was sliding shut, and that was all she cared about. Getting as far away from this floor as possible. She'd get out at the next stop and hide out in the stairwell. At least she knew from experience that there, she'd be guaranteed some privacy until she was capable of hiding her shattered heart from public eyes.

Before the door shut completely, there was a shout out in the hall.

No, no, no. Don't do this to me.

One of the men instinctively threw out a hand in front of the slider so that the door jerked to a stop and started back the other way. "No!" she cried. "Let it close, please."

He'd obviously picked up on her distressed state and took his hand away again. The elevator door hesitated but started to close again.

Too late.

Ben's hand, followed by his sculpted, still *bare* arm, snaked inside the elevator to stop the door. Desperate to disappear, she squeezed past the other passengers until her heels hit the back of the elevator.

Her mouth dropped open. He'd come after her without changing, without even putting on a pair of shoes.

Both of the women gasped as he filled the entrance, holding the hotel-sized towel around his waist with just one fisted hand. The edge barely reached the tops of his muscular thighs and spread apart at the bottom. Water still dripped from his tousled hair and tracked over his naked shoulders and chest, down his torso, and beneath the edge of the towel.

"Beth!"

"Oh God," she murmured, devastated. She just wanted to lick her wounds in private.

"Dude," one guy said with a grin. "You want to go get dressed and do...whatever this is with the lady later?"

"Stay out of it," he snapped, slapping his palm flat against the door when it tried to shut on him again. "Beth, come back out."

His pecs flexed as he stretched to find her way in the back. She peered through the break in the bodies standing between them. He was the most magnificent thing she'd ever seen.

And he was about to lose that towel.

One of the women in the elevator leaned in close. "If you're not going to go with him, I will," she whispered.

Liz's lips twitched, but she crossed her arms. "You made yourself pretty clear, Ben. What do you want?"

"You!" His jaw clenched as their gazes locked. "Of course I want you. I've always wanted you."

"Really?" Hope bloomed.

"Would I be out here in the hallway of the hotel naked, holding up a packed elevator, if I wasn't serious?" Exasperation tinged his voice, but there was laughter in his eyes.

"Then why would you make me go through that back there? You all but threw me out of your room."

"Seriously, dude?" The one guy piped up again. "That's not cool, man. I would never—"

"I didn't throw her out," he snarled with impatience, a telling flush crawling down his neck to his chest. "I just… damn it, Beth. I was hurt, and it was instinct for me to try to protect myself so it couldn't happen again. But I knew as soon as you ran out the door that I'd made a horrible mistake. I don't want to protect myself from you. You're the one person I know I can be vulnerable with. I knew it yesterday, and nothing's changed today."

A high-pitched beeping sound interrupted them. It was the elevator, probably getting pissy because the door had been held open for so long.

"Beth, please come out," he said.

Every single person in the elevator turned to look at her with expectant expressions. She bit her lip.

The elevator started to beep louder. "That's the alarm," someone said. "This door's gotta close now, or security'll be up here to investigate."

Reluctantly, Ben let go of the elevator and took a step back. She looked into his eyes, filled with a naked honesty, forgiveness, and so much love.

"Let me out. Don't let the door close," she said urgently, pushing her way back to the front as quickly as she could, her heart filled to bursting.

The two women started clapping, and one of the guys hooted as Liz threw herself at Ben and reached around his neck to kiss him. The door started closing again just as he put both arms around her...and let go of the towel.

The sound of the security alarm and the startled gasps of their audience were cut off as the elevator finally closed.

When he finally lifted his head, he smoothed the hair back from her face and smiled softly. "Want to give me your jacket?"

She giggled. "No way."

"Come on, I'm naked here." His grin twisted. "And I forgot to grab a passkey before I left the hotel room."

She shook with laughter, until it was hard to breathe. "You'll have to make do with the itty-bitty towel." She opened her coat and showed him why.

"You're not wearing anything under there!" He snapped the jacket tightly closed and looked over her shoulder.

That only made her laugh harder.

If she'd learned anything this week, it was that *some* spontaneity and reckless behavior was good for a person. It kept the blood pumping and the soul alive.

Yeah, she could do this.

"Jesus," he muttered. "When you decide to embrace recklessness, you really go all out, don't you?"

"That was the idea," she said. "But I think you just took the cake coming after me the way you did."

He laughed. "Please tell me that you have your room

key with you."

She nodded. He bent and grabbed his towel, and they quickly retreated back down the hall to her room.

Inside, he slammed the door shut and pressed her up against the wall, tossing the scrap of terrycloth and pushing her coat off her shoulders to the floor. She groaned and tipped her head back. The air conditioners still weren't working because of the storm, and the heat of his body was sticky against her bare skin.

"Wait," she murmured, her hand against his chest. "You're getting on a plane to New York in, what? A couple of hours? How are we going to make this work after we leave paradise? I need to know we have a plan."

With such gentleness she could cry, he cupped her face in his hands. "Is that the only thing you're worried about?"

She nodded. "I think I managed to work the rest out on my own."

"Baby, that's going to be the easy part. We'll find a way," he promised with a kiss. "Don't you think with our two brilliant minds put together we'll be able to figure out a simple matter of geography?"

"And, you think you can handle...handle your girlfriend being your company's biggest competition?" Oh God, thinking was impossible now. The look in his eyes was smoking, as if he had already planned out all the things he was going to do to her body.

He leaned over her until his mouth was just a hairsbreadth away from hers. "It will definitely keep things interesting," he murmured, tugging her bottom lip between his teeth, then soothing the tiny bite with his tongue.

She pressed her chest against his, trying to contain the

ache spreading through her.

"But since we're all about taking risks now, don't think you'll be able to avoid a merger forever…on both personal and professional levels." His kiss was deeper this time, drugging and sweet.

"I suppose I might be persuaded to entertain proposals." She couldn't get enough of him, her gaze following her trembling hands over every dip and curve and plane of his muscled body, as he did the same to her.

"I thought you might." His eyes sparkled as he lifted her right off the ground into his arms. "But don't worry, I have no doubt we'll find a creative way to negotiate terms."

Suddenly she felt like laughing because it was hard to contain such joy and happiness. More than that, she felt hope and confidence, that what they had together was good and strong, and that it could really last. That it could grow into something even more precious.

"First, I seem to remember another promise you made that has yet to be fulfilled."

He stopped short, his expression turning quizzical. "What promise is that?"

"You promised we'd do it up against the wall."

She did laugh then, and when his booming laugh mingled with hers, she wrapped her arms around his neck and held on tight, ready for the adventure of her life.

Acknowledgments

I love the moment when a book is really, truly finished. Not the day that I write the last word on the last page of my first draft—a book is never finished on that day—I'm talking about the day when all the revising, editing, polishing, scheduling, cover art, and other behind-the-scenes work is done. Because after the first draft (sometimes the second or third), that's when the book gets into the hands of all the people who really make the story shine, and that's why I want to say thank you to a whole bunch of wonderful people now.

First and foremost, thank you to all the readers, bloggers, and reviewers out there. You are why I do this! You make "coming into work each day" a JOY, and it's my dream to be able to write more stories for you all to enjoy, so I want to hear from you!

Of course, I want to thank my husband and son, who support my dreams in so many ways. It's about more than ignoring the piles of laundry when I'm on deadline, or remembering everything that I forget. It's about the sacrifices we make together, and the future we plan together. Thank you so much! I can never express how much it means to me to have you in my corner.

And to my talented critique partners, the people who aren't afraid to tell me when I've lost my focus and help get me back on track. They are there each and every day to keep me going, and are the dearest friends I could ever ask for: Christine, Kim, Amy, and Paula.

This book would not be what it is without the invaluable knowledge, assistance, and guidance of three very important people: Tracy Montoya, Kate Fall, and Alethea Spiridon Hopson. I'm so grateful to be working with you all.

And to all the other fantastic people at Entangled Publishing and especially with the Indulgence line, who work so hard to bring out the best in us authors, including (but certainly not limited to) Heather Howland, Liz Pelletier, Heather Riccio, Debbie Suzuki, and Melanie Smith.

About the Author

J.K. Coi is a multi-published, award-winning author of contemporary and paranormal romance and urban fantasy. She makes her home in Ontario, Canada, with her husband and son and a feisty black cat who is the uncontested head of the household. While she spends her days immersed in the litigious world of insurance law, she is very happy to spend her nights writing dark and sexy characters who leap off the page and into readers' hearts.

Find her online at www.jkcoi.com, and visit her alter ego, Chloe Jacobs, who writes thrilling dark fantasy for young adults (www.chloejacobs.com).

Made in the USA
Charleston, SC
10 November 2014